THE BURDENS OF TEN WOMEN

THE BURDENS OF TEN WOMEN

By I. C. Ozed-Williams. FOTTBanner 2009

AUTHOR: I. C. OZED-WILLIAMS

© 2009 by FOTT Banner Productions
P. O Box 213, Linthicum. MD 21090
e-mail: icozedwilliams@gmail.com

DEDICATION

To all my patients:
Those who have attained,
And those still in the place of prayer
We shall never give up hoping…

HOPE MAKETH NOT ASHAMED

PREFACE

Babies are so important especially in the environment we live. We use them to mark health, mark wealth, and to mark prowess. All the major religions of the world recognize having babies as a blessing. Even atheists see them as relevant to propagating the future. It is very distressing therefore for any couple to be unable to have a child especially when they so sincerely desire to have one, whereas others who do not want to have (at least at a particular time) keep getting pregnant. Over and over, this author has heard litanies like, "I see no reason why if I kept getting pregnant as a young schoolgirl, unready to be a mother, I cannot get pregnant now that I sincerely desire to do so!" Or "Why can't God take and give to those that have been praying for pregnancy. Why me? Why now?"

For a woman to become pregnant, a normal sperm must travel in the company of millions of other sperm cells, through a normal male genital tract, into a normal female genital tract, to meet and fertilize a normal egg and then travel back through a normal fallopian tube into a normal womb and there be incubated! Even when all conditions are equal, as the Economists would say, this process has only a 12 to 22 percent chance of succeeding in any given month for any couple that have been having sexual intercourse of at least three to four times per week. This means that everything may be normal: sperms, egg, genital tracts, womb, temperature, pressure etcetera; and yet a couple stand a seventy-eight to eighty-eight percent chance of not getting pregnant in any month.

The wonder is that so many people achieve it. The question remains about why schoolgirls jump the wall for just one night of adventure and come back pregnant? Why does one incident of rape or assault results in the conception of a baby? Why are some women just "Touch-and-go"? Why do some other women try all the contraceptive methods within their reach and still keep getting pregnant?

On the other hand, are people that have sex all the time and yet do not get pregnant. There are people that use all the modern and often expensive contraptions known to man and still do not get pregnant! Surely, chance cannot account for all this. Science must acknowledge that the finger of God continues to operate in the affairs of men. Some of us still firmly believe that every conception is special. No baby is ever a "Mistake" because God does not make mistakes.

However, this book is about those that really tried and desired to get pregnant but did not. The stories chosen here are by no means because they are the commonest, nor the rarest. They are chosen because the reason the couples have for not realizing their dreams are often too obvious and therefore often overlooked. Simple lifestyle changes can often prevent, and sometimes correct what is being seen as a big problem. In real life sometimes, the problem often has more than one root-cause. Seeing a doctor often helps to crystallize the problem though not all can be solved – yet! For the first time, in talking to a doctor, couples begin to see problems they had not realized that they had, and hopefully realize there are solutions to many of them.

This book is not merely for those who want to have babies or are struggling with such issues. It is also for:

- Those who are involved in bringing up young boys and girls that will eventually become the parents of tomorrow.
- People who are involved with counseling such people at different levels, mentally and spiritually.
- The merely curious who wish to increase their knowledge. There is no end to learning.
- The health worker or the casual helper who may not realize that their action or lack of it may affect someone's future forever.
- Finally, it is for everybody because we all have just the one body each. We cannot exchange it. Let us learn how to take care of this body so that it can serve us well, and for long.

Happy Reading!

FOREWORD

Dr. Ozed-Williams has written a significant and practical exposition on the common causes of infertility especially in this part of the world. The illustrations in this book are helpful, well-constructed and emphatically make the point. Throughout the book, there is a humane thought of the people, the community they live in and their cultural background. The sensitive and the compassionate discussion of each case after each story also enriches the knowledge of the reader.

One must also appreciate the emphasis on the epidemiology and the available medical treatment of infertility at the end of the book. It is a well-honed and a quick approach to this aspect of infertility. Good attention has been given to the overwhelming effect of unsafe abortions and sexually transmissible infections and there is no doubt that this adds to the practicality of the book.

This book is directed to the generality of our mostly uninformed or at best poorly informed population. It is a compendium of information, and I am excited and enthused by its broad expanse. Reading this book is like going on a long journey with a very knowledgeable tour guide and writing this foreword has been a very great privilege.

Adebiyi Gbadebo Adesiyun
Professor and Head, Infertility Unit
Obstetrics & Gynaecology Department
Ahmadu Bello University Teaching Hospital
Shika-Zaria

Contents

FAVOURS UNLIMITED

*N*obody could quite say for sure if Sale was a doctor, but everyone called him that. He had come to their remote village and set up a hospital. This was quite a relief to the villagers for whom the nearest hospital was the government hospital over twenty-five kilometers away. They could only get to the hospital by bus on market days, or by bicycle on other days for those who were lucky enough to own bicycles or to know someone that could lend them one. If someone was sick enough, they formed a bush ambulance. This is a long piece of cotton cloth stretched between two long poles. This was carried by four men at each end. Four other men would walk along these, ready to take over when the first set got exhausted. Alternating in this way, they eventually got to the hospital often too exhausted to even speak; and often too late to save the patient. If the patient was still alive, then would follow the difficulty of getting the hospital personnel to even look at them. These latter often started by berating them very harshly for not getting the patient to hospital on time. They reprimanded the villagers for their ignorant and stupid ways.

The very thought of going to the hospital often filled the villagers with trepidation. It was often easier to leave the sick person to die more peacefully at home. However, when they lingered so much over dying, the consciences of their relatives, friends and neighbors would be pricked. They would once again brave the journey, often with the same results. Few survived. These came home again. Some were healthy and restored. Others were permanently marred for life, physically, emotionally, or very often economically. These were few enough, and so they mostly chose to manage as their ancestors before them had done: with herbs and what the medicine man could rustle up. They left the rest to fate.

And then came Sale. Later rumors had it that Sale was fleeing from a scandal in a city and was looking for a remote village to hide away. He brought a lot of relief to the people. At first, he rented two rooms. And then as his business grew, he bought a piece of land and built his own place. It was just a long mud hut with many rooms where he ran out-patient clinics, admitted the occasional patient, conducted labors, and had his own living quarters. He gave employment to some of the village girls, to whom he taught basic hygiene. He always had them scrub and keep the hospital gleaming, and the beds with their thin mattresses dressed in white sheets. There were blue curtains on the windows and blue drapes on the tables. The place was more upbeat than any hut in the village and smelt of antiseptics like the government hospital did. Sale could speak their language. The medications he gave them were far neater, less disagreeable, and worked faster than that of the medicine man.

True, some women died in childbirth at Sale's place, but these would have died on the way to the government hospital anyway. Besides, look at the ones who did not die, and could have died if Sale was not there. True, some children also died at Sale's place but many more were saved, and a lot less were dying since Sale came.

In the same way, when there were rumors of Sale's carryings-on with the village girls, the parents of the girls or the girls themselves were blamed rather than Sale. Everyone agreed that Sale was a great help to the village. They tried not to offend him and drive him away. Sale appeared humble on the outside, but he knew the privileged position he had among these people. He tried to be discreet, but he nevertheless went out of his to have himself a good time. That was before the event of Godiya.

Godiya was born about the time Sale came to live in the village. When she was about eight years old, she had come from playing with her friends to the grass-roofed house which she shared with her parents and her younger brother. She saw people gathered in front of the hut while it burnt merrily in the dry crisp Harmattan wind. The origin of the fire was not known but there was already a waterline formed from the river trying to quench it. Everyone knew that it was useless. They could hear the cries of the inhabitants of the hut for some time, but no one dared to go in. The heat was too intense.

When Godiya came to the scene she took in everything that was happening. With a blood-curdling yell, she was about to fling herself into the fire, but strong arms held her back. Everything, and everyone burnt to ashes. Godiya alone had survived from that family of four, and that, by a quirk of fate. She became a wreck. It was heart-rending to see so much grief in one so very little girl. She moved about with bowed shoulders and was forever looking downwards as if for a lost coin.

At first some friendly neighbors took her in while attempts were made to locate her relatives. The ones that were contacted were either "Too far away to take her" or "Too uncomfortable where they were to take another person in". Some were "Too many already in one household to make an addition". Nobody really wanted Godiya until Mama Ladi took her in.

Mama Ladi had been a widow for such a long time that nobody really remembered who her husband was. She had no surviving children and though everyone called her Mama Ladi, none of them was really a near-of-kin. Her real name was not even Mama Ladi. No one really knew what her real name was. She was just called Mama Ladi (Sunday Mother) because she seemed to be in charge of everything that happened at the church. She took care of strangers that came to the church for anything, and anyone that was ostracized from the community especially for church-related matters was sure to find refuge in her house. It was therefore almost natural and to be expected that Mama Ladi would take Godiya in when nobody else seemed to want her.

It took time but the little girl began to smile again. She never went back to being the lively, boisterous, mischievous girl that she was before the fire but she began to live again. She was of a very sweet disposition and wore such a wise look as only those who had looked into the depths of pain could wear. She loved everyone and everyone loved her back.

Mama Ladi worked hard to raise the money and sent her to a Christian Boarding School. When she came home during the holidays, they always had a very joyful re-union. At thirteen Godiya began to menstruate. Mama Ladi taught her all that a mother should and warned her that the periods could sometimes be painful. She told her what to do if this ever happened.

For over a year, Godiya menstruated without pains. The pains, when they started, were just enough to make her squeeze her face from time to time. Over time, the pains continued to gradually increase until she could hardly bear it. The school nurse had to prescribe some medications to enable her at least live a close to a normal life as possible. Soon, Godiya began to live in anticipation of the pains each month. "It's so terrible Mamee" she told Mama Ladi. "Everybody now knows when I am menstruating, including the teachers. It's so embarrassing."

Mama Ladi comforted her with the little knowledge she had, and added, "They say that it gets better after one's first baby."

"But I am only fifteen now Mamee. I'm not yet thinking of marriage, not to talk of babies!" They had laughed together companionably. They were that intimate.

But the pain continued. Each month was an agony to the poor young girl. Her best friend at school, Saratu, told her one day "Some people say that when you have sex the pain reduces."

"They say! They say!" Godiya retorted scornfully. "Doctors without certificates! Is there anything people won't say?"

"But it is true!" said a girl who just happened to be passing by. Lanti was not a friend of theirs. In fact, she had a very bad reputation. Her offences included things like blatant rudeness to teachers, skipping classes, and she had even been known to jump over the fence on an occasion or two. She was also a profligate liar, so much so that a teacher once said of her, "If Lanti bids you a good afternoon, you better check that the sun is still shining."

She was never good news. Butting into their conversation now, she said, "Take me as an example. I used to have very painful periods until I had sex for the first time. Phiam! (She snapped her fingers) the pains just started reducing. After six months of sex, I could hardly tell when I was menstruating again. It just minds its own business and I mind mine."

Now everything that she said were lies but Lanti enjoyed telling long tales and watching their effects on her hearers. Godiya and Saratu just stared at her and did not continue their discussion nor try to include her in any way. After some time Lanti just shrugged and moved away muttering to herself with a smile, "At least I did try to be friendly."

"Don't believe anything that girl says" Saratu said as Lanti moved away. "She only deals in lies."

"But you were just advising me along such lines yourself just now" Godiya reminded her.

"Yes," admitted Saratu "but we both knew that we were just joking."

"I don't know about that" said Godiya flippantly, "Mamee also said something like that to me once."

"She said that you should have sex to stop menstrual pain?" Saratu asked incredulous.

"No" Godiya recanted, "She said that the pains usually reduce after one's first baby."

"So, you'd like to have your first baby now. Now? And as a cure for your pains?"

"Well," Godiya said frowning in concentration and speaking in the meditative manner that told Saratu that she was considering something very seriously, "maybe Mamee doesn't know it all; or knows but is not telling me everything because she doesn't want me to...to…"

"Don't even go there Godiya," Saratu said suddenly alarmed, "Don't even think about it."

But Saratu was not the one who used to suffer through the monthly pains. In addition to the pains, Godiya now also started vomiting on the first day as well. Her breasts would swell and be painful for about a week before the blood finally started flowing and her face would be filled with very painful pimples. The thought of these happening month after month after month was just too much to bear.

When in school, the school nurse always gave Godiya something for the pains. During the holidays however, she suffered much trying herbal teas, warm compresses, and any other thing that Mama Ladi managed to rustle up. Finally, the day came when she felt that she could not take it anymore. Mama Ladi was at church supervising the weekly cleaning up. Godiya decided to go and see Sale. Sale just gave her one injection. Within minutes she was feeling relieved enough to chat.

"And is this what I will be seeing monthly for the rest of my life?" She asked woefully.

"Not for the rest of your life Sale said soothingly. "When you become an old woman you will not be menstruating anymore, and of course when you are pregnant you will not be menstruating."

Both were quiet for a while thinking their own separate thoughts. And then, seeming to make up her mind, Godiya asked in a rushed voice, "Is it true that having sex relieves this kind of pain?"

"What?" Sale asked, startled out of his own reverie. Godiya repeated her question. Having really heard it the second time, and having had time to consider it, Sale answered "Yes! Yes! It happens like that at times".

And then Sale committed the heinous crime that started his downfall. "I can do it for you if you want" he offered.

They both laughed self-consciously and Godiya left. After that, whenever they met at the market, the church, or other public places he would give her a leering look and ask out of the corner of his mouth, "Still looking for a permanent solution to those pains?"

Godiya would quickly look away, but the seeds were sown. They were watered by those monthly pains and by the secrecy that she allowed to shroud it all. She did not discuss it with Mama Ladi, nor yet with Saratu at school. She did ask Lanti of all people, though. "If I had sex to stop these menstrual pains, how many times would I need to do it?"

"Oh," Lanti answered, "Mine disappeared after the first time but I found out that I enjoyed having sex. I just continued doing it in order to make assurance doubly sure. Those menstrual pains never recurred."

Lies, all lies! In fact, Lanti was still a virgin because the boys were afraid of her brazen attitude. However, Godiya wanted someone to tell her those lies so she swallowed it all – hook, line and sinker like a baited fish. The next time that she was on holidays she went to offer her help to Sale. She knew very well that Mama Ladi would not approve. She held people while he gave them injections. She washed up the instruments he had used for the day and tidied away the left-over medications and injections. She swept up the place after the last patient had gone, and still sat on in the waiting room.

Sale read the signs correctly. He was only too willing to comply. He did not rape her. He only took what was offered to him. She did not enjoy the sex. She told herself that hopefully, the menstrual pains would be cured. That month, she did not see her period at all even though it had been as regular as clockwork before then. It was when it had passed by about two weeks, and she began to feel sickly that she panicked. They had been told all about it at school and she was over sixteen years after all.

She went to see Sale. "I think you have made me pregnant" she blurted out to him.

"That is not possible after only one encounter" he said. "Anyway, find an excuse to come to town next market day and I will find out if you are really pregnant."

Godiya did not know on what pretext to go into town the next market day. Finally, she told Mama Ladi that a school project required her to gather some information from town. Mama Ladi believed her. Godiya never gave anyone reason to be suspicious of her movements.

In town, Godiya thought that her blood or her urine sample would just be taken for testing, but this did not happen at all. It turned out that Sale had a friend with an unpleasant wolfish grin. This friend explained to Godiya, "I will just flush your womb and cause your menses to resume normally again."

"But that is abortion!" Godiya protested.

"Not really" Sale explained smoothly. "Abortion is if the baby has formed. Even if you are pregnant, which I doubt very much, it will just be a clot of blood now and not a definite human being."

Godiya was still hesitant. Nevertheless, she agreed to at least have Sale's friend check her. He took her arm and gave her an injection that caused her to sleep off immediately. She awoke with a throbbing pain between her legs and cramps in her lower abdomen. It was like ten menstrual pains in one. When she groaned as she tried to get up, Sale and his friend hovered over her asking if all was well. She assured them that all was not well. "My head is swimming. My legs are aching. I cannot stand on my legs. They set up an infusion of a clear fluid for her. Both of them watched over her like a mother hen. By evening, Sale insisted that she got on the bus going back to the village. He supported her to Mama Ladi's house and said that he had found her in town looking sick; and had given her some medications. Mama Ladi was profuse in her thanks. Godiya could hardly talk and just collapsed into bed.

About midnight Mama Ladi was woken up by loud groans coming from Godiya's room. She lit a lamp and went to the girl's room to find her rolling on the ground in pain. When she came nearer, she saw that all her clothes were soaked in blood. "I'm dying Mamee. I know I am going to die."

Alarmed, Mama Ladi tried to reassure her that she would not die. "Let me wake our neighbors up to go for Sale."

"No Mamee, not Sale. It has to do with him too. I know that God is punishing me for what I did. I was foolish Mamee."

Mama Ladi tried to tear herself away and go for help, but the girl held her with surprising strength. She wanted Mama Ladi to know everything that had transpired in case she died. "I'm so sorry Mamee. I'm so sorry. I have sinned against you and against God. Please say that you forgive me Mamee."

Mama Ladi now understood why Godiya had not wanted her to send for Sale, but the girl needed help. "Okay," she said. "I forgive you. I'm sure God forgives you too."

"Thank you Mamee" Godiya said, and then she sank back on the ground unconscious. Mama Ladi raised a piercing wail that woke the entire village. They heard the story in bits from her, and then confirmed that Sale had "helped" enough of the other village girls in that way. This was the last straw that broke the camel's back. Immediately, the villagers divided themselves into two: one half immediately formed a bush ambulance that carried the unconscious girl back to the city, to the government hospital. The other half went as a man to go and set fire to Sale's place. Sale had woken up with the rest of the village when Mama Ladi screamed. He quickly gathered the gist of what was happening. Knowing himself to be the villain of the drama, he had gone back to his house, put a few things together and was on the run again, perhaps to another remote village.

Godiya recovered but her adventure became the subject of open discussion, even in her school. It also worsened her menstrual pain so that the pain began about a full week before the menses and lasted for up to two days afterwards. She graduated, went on to study nursing and midwifery. She returned to the village afterwards to repair and reopen Sale's place in order to serve her people. She tells all her suitors, "I'm not sure that I will ever have a baby because of the foolishness of my youth."

She was quite frank about it. All of her suitors went away except for Musa. Musa had three children from his dead wife and was believing God that a miracle could happen for him and Godiya. With Mama Ladi's blessing, they have been married for ten years now. They are still waiting for that miracle otherwise they are very happy with each other and with what they are doing.

FAVOURS

Many foolish girls lose their virginity on false premises such as "Others are doing it"; "It could cure menstrual pain"; "It proves one really loves a boy"; and so on. Sometimes their friends who encourage this have not gone that way themselves at all. They are either good story tellers or good motivational speakers. The truth also remains that those that allow themselves to be persuaded into it really wanted to do so somewhere in their hearts. They were just looking for "a reasonable excuse" to jump into it. Most girls are not forced to do it, they chose to do it.

But does sex really cure menstrual pains?

*That is a myth, absolutely false! However, most myths are built on some elements of truth. Mama Ladi was right. Many people **(but not all)** that have severe menstrual pain tend to feel better after their first childbirth. How this happens is not well-known, but the experts feel that this might have to do with the dilatation of the mouth of the womb which occurs as part of childbirth. However, artificially dilating this mouth of the womb has not achieved the same results and is not that beneficial for treating menstrual pains.*

The truth about the matter really is that having engaged in illicit sex most girls then tend to develop the pains of infection in addition to the basic menstrual pain (see Pre-nuptial Lessons). Some unfortunate ones like Godiya become pregnant in addition and go on to have babies when they are not fully ready. Some still worsen their situation by trying to get an abortion. Godiya's pains were short and predictable before the event but afterwards it became worse and longer-lasting so one tends to ask, "Was it all really worth it?"

Are there medications that control menstrual pain?

Definitely! And some work better than others; and some people react to some groups of medications better than to other groups. What Sale gave to Godiya seemed to work for her better than what the school nurse had been giving her. What a sensible person would have done would have been to get the prescription and use it more often.

The side-effects of Godiya's misadventure were prolongation of the pains, and later inability to have babies. Some other more lethal side-effects have included perforation of the womb, the bladder or the intestines. Some people have been known to bleed to death; some others develop raging infections that affect the reproductive organs, the blood, and other major organs like the kidneys, the liver, the heart and even the brain! This author knows a few people that developed mental problems from this.

It is better not to enter this type of thing and ruin one's future than to rush in like a fool to a place where angels fear to tread!

PRE-NUPTIAL LESSONS

"*Y*ou are too serious! Can't you even take a joke?"

This was something that Ifu kept hearing over and over, when he was a child, as he grew into a youth, and now as a young man. He often wondered at it himself too. It was not really as if he could not take a joke or laugh with, or like other people. He also felt that the business of life and of living required some measure of seriousness. He would often respond to most things beginning with, "You are not serious, let us not joke about this…"

Even his parents wondered at his seriousness. His father often said philosophically, "At least he will make a devotedly serious husband for some lucky girl someday."

"That is, if he ever loosens up enough to even approach a girl to ask her to marry him" his mother would often retort.

But he did approach a girl. She did agree to become his wife to the surprise and envy of most of his friends. Ifu had become an accountant. He took and passed his professional examinations at just a sitting each. He had a choice of who to work for out of all the big companies that wanted him. On top of all that, he had landed Nife as a wife. Nife, whom everyone had wanted and tried getting but had failed! His friends begrudged Ifu the good job he had, and the first-rate wife he was getting. Perhaps there was value to that entire serious outlook to life afer all.

Nife was brilliant. She was sparkling. She was beautiful. She was from a good home, and she had a wonderful heart. She was very pious and devout. Even Ifu's "Bad

Friends" could vouch that she was still a virgin. This was no second-hand wife, and she had agreed to marry Ifu of all people! Nobody could tell how this had come to be, but it was happening under their very noses.

The wedding day was fixed. The bridesmaids and the groomsmen had all been selected and kitted out. The cake had been baked and decorated. The caterers all knew their roles and even the extra things that were expected of them. Response to the invitation had been spectacular. From far and near, friends, relatives, colleagues, old school friends, and even casual acquaintances were coming. Most of the excitement of weddings after all was the hectic days spent planning and anticipating it.

Ifu's friends had also planned for it. "Come on," they urged "you deserve a bachelor's eve party to send you off."

Ifu was not sure that he wanted a bachelor's eve party. He had attended one in the past and did not find it amusing. "These people are not serious" had been his comment then, and now also, to his friends.

"Loosen up a bit for once," they persisted. "One is young only once, and we pray this is the only time that you will ever marry. We pray that your marriage to Nife will be long and fulfilling. Come on, let us give you this good time for once. We have carefully planned and invested reasonably in it."

What did one say to such goodwill? They were right. This was a once-in-a-lifetime event where he was the chief celebrant and had center stage. Besides, they had gone to all that trouble and spent all that money to set it all up. The least that he could do was allow himself to be persuaded to loosen up for a few hours and enjoy himself.

Ifu's friends had spent money alright. The party held at a hotel across town. There were a lot of alcoholic beverages, but they had made allowances for the celebrant who was a teetotaler. They had also provided fruit punches. Ifu was glad for this consideration. What he did not know was that the punches were very subtly laced with alcohol. Afterwards he admitted that even this was not an excuse for what followed.

He tried very hard to enjoy the party, but the room was too hot and over-crowded. The music was too loud and throbbing. The company was so totally not serious at all. He could have thought of a thousand more acceptable ways to spend his last night as a bachelor. By midnight they sang him the popular send-off song: "Farewell to bachelorhood. From tomorrow I have a Missus."

"We have a special gift for you," announced one of his friends.

By now Ifu was quite tipsy, and his speech had become slurred. Nevertheless, he managed to ask, "And what is this special gift that cannot wait for the reception tomorrow?"

"Later today you moron!" corrected one of his friends.

"It's a gift for now" the first speaker explained. "It's a girl. It would not do to have you come to your wedding bed tomorrow still a virgin. You would not even know where to poke your thing into."

The other friends joined in a raucous laughter. It was true that at thirty Ifu was still a virgin. He made no secret of that fact. "It's unserious people that go philandering about before they are married. After marriage I shall get all the sex that I want," had been his steadfast philosophy. At his bachelor's eve party, he also replied, "Go away! I don't need that kind of gift now. I shall make all the discoveries that I need tomorrow."

"Not tomorrow, today!" he was corrected again but his wits were not about him. Before he was aware of what was happening, he had been bundled into a darkened room. All he could make out was the silhouette of a naked woman on a bed. Before he could take it all in, she was firmly undressing him. She kissed him, touching him in erotic places. He was a red-blooded man after all. He lacked his usual control over himself in his tipsy state. He was never quite sure of what followed afterwards. He woke up in bright daylight with a deep sense of guilt, revulsion, and self-loathing. The deed was done. It was irrevocable. He was expected to star at a wedding a few hours from thence. His friends hurried him off home to shower and dress, and also to harbor a dark secret that he knew he would never share with his bride.

The wedding went like a dream. Everything went perfectly according to all the planning. There were lots of toasts to the bride and the groom praising their virginity. "And very soon, we shall begin to see the fruits of their patience." Everybody chorused a loud "Amen!"

Ifu felt so guilty at all these false commendations, but he fought it down. He had apologized to God. He had severely reprimanded his so-called friends. He now knew them for what they really were. Surely this was all over. God forgives sins after all.

The wedding night left nothing to be desired on either side. Sex was all that they had imagined it to be and all that they had heard that it was. They took no precautions against getting pregnant. They rather hoped that it would happen to them sooner rather than later.

A few days after wedding, Nife complained to her mother that she had a burning sensation whenever she passed urine. "It's normal" her mother reassured her. "It happens when someone starts having sex for the first time. Just take a lot of water. If the pain is much, take Aspirin and avoid sex for a few days."

Obedient daughter that she was, and since her mother had never misled her, Nife complied. The pain stopped and she forgot all about it.

Ifu had also been experiencing burning sensation on passing urine. What was more, he also noticed that something like pus was coming out of the tip of his penis. He was worldly-wise enough to know that this was the dreaded gonorrhea, and that he did not catch it from his wife. He went to a chemist far away from his house and his office and simply told the man there, "I think I may have a sex disease. Please mix some medications for me."

The Chemist complied but then asked, "What of your girlfriend? Should I mix medications for her too?" He was a man of the world and knew such things happened from time to time.

Ifu was startled but he shook his head vehemently and said almost with a shout, "No! No! I have no girlfriend. It was only a one-night affair. She is not my girlfriend at all."

The chemist was startled. He had not asked for a confessional. The man was probably telling the truth. He took note of the wedding ring on Ifu's finger and understood most of what must have happened. "Okay! Okay!" he mollified Ifu as he gave him the medications and received his payment. Ifu left.

Ifu felt better with the medications. He was also glad that Nife was better on her mother's recommendations, and he thought that was the end of the matter. After a few days, they resumed having sex. Some days later, his symptoms came back: the pain, the pus, everything just as before. Nife herself had no complaints except that her period had come just on time as expected and she was very disappointed that she was not yet pregnant. She was getting used to sex in her marriage and had nothing to complain about in that wise.

Ifu went back to the same Chemist he had seen before. "I thought you said it was a one-night affair." He asked Ifu.

"It was," Ifu affirmed strongly.

"I can't understand why the problem returned. Did you take the medications the way I told you to?"

"I did everything exactly as you asked me to" Ifu insisted.

"Hmm! This is very curious." The chemist frowned, puzzled but he filled out the prescription as at the last time. Ifu took time to learn the names of the medications and their dosages so that if he needed them again, he did not have to come back to the same inquisitive chemist.

Over the next few months, he did have need of those medications. He would take them and feel better for some time. However, once he had sex with his wife the problem would start again after a few days. He never mentioned it to anyone, not even to Nife but in private he cried to God and agonized: "O God, it was only for one night, and even then, I was manipulated into it. Won't you for the sake of the years that I kept myself chaste and sensible forgive this one simple error and take away this reproach, this disease?"

The next time he went to get the medications, the woman at the counter noticed the ring and said to him, "I don't know why you are taking these medications, but don't you think you should see a doctor and have your wife treated as well?"

His wife! At the back of his mind, he had always suspected so too but he had squashed it. The other chemist had talked of his girlfriend being treated. That was easy, he had none but how was he going to confront his wife with this evidence of his past error and foolishness? He could tell her a cock-and-bull story, "We were told at work today that this medication would be good for husband and wife together…" That did not sound plausible even in his own ears.

Or "I bumped into Mama Ngoo today and she said that two of us should take these medications, that it will enhance our fertility…" or perhaps, "One of the wives at work said that you should take these medications for those symptoms you were having soon after the wedding…"

None of them sounded reasonable. If they must take medications, why don't they go and see a doctor first. That would be more in keeping with Ifu's nature. Lying and deception were not in his nature at all. The pharmacist was right. They ought to go to see a doctor together. He just had to work up the courage that it would take to tell her.

Fate took it right out of his hands. He came back and met his wife groaning and rolling on the floor in pains. "It's menstrual cramps" she bit out through teeth gritted for pain.

"It's been gradually getting worse over the past few months but today is so bad. I just can't bear it."

He did not even wait to try anything. He just quickly got her into the car and drove to the hospital as fast as he could. She was instantly admitted and commenced on drips and injections. In a private moment, Ifu took the doctor aside and confided in him about the medications he had been taking, and the adventure that he had the night before his wedding. "I don't know if it has anything to do with what my wife is going through now, and should I continue on the medications anyway?"

The doctor was sympathetic rather than judgmental. He simply wondered why Ifu did not think to give to his wife too after taking it more than once. Ifu admitted his guilt and shame. He confided that he was that very day trying to work up the courage to do so until it was overtaken by events. The doctor asked him to continue on the medications but added a few more injections. "We are treating your wife with these too. What you told me is a great help in managing her. Thank you. Two of you will be okay."

Nife became well and was discharged. Her periods were no longer painful. For Ifu, sex became less of an ordeal, and they lived together happily except that they did not yet have a baby. A year passed, then two. At the end of that time, Nife went to the hospital to enquire. She was asked a lot of questions including how many times she had sex in a week. Were her menses painful? Had she ever been treated for infection in the past? What contraceptive method had she ever used?

"You are asking about a Family planning method?" she asked incredulously. "I'm trying to have babies, not stop them from coming!"

A battery of tests was ordered for her: swabs, x-rays, ultrasounds and even some blood tests. That was when she learnt that more than one type of test could be done with the blood. She was asked for up to five different types!

Some of the tests were quite expensive but she was not looking at costs. If she could be assured that a baby awaited her after it all, it would be money more than well-spent. "If you told me to sell all we have and get a baby at the end of it all, I probably will" she told the doctor.

After all these tests for her, only one was ordered for Ifu. Ifu was to come for semen analysis. "I hope he will agree to come. Many husbands do not agree to come."

"Oh, he will come alright," Nife assured the doctor confidently. "He wants a baby just as much as I do."

"That's nice," said the doctor. "Perhaps you should come together when we discuss the test results so we can plot a course of treatment together as a team."

Nife saw to it that all the tests were done, including Ifu's own. She also saw to it that the results came out on time for the conference with the doctor. Some of the tests were uncomfortable; some were very painful. Nife bore it all. "Oh Lord, let us have a baby at the end of it all" she prayed whenever she found it difficult to go on.

The period they waited for their turn to see the doctor was among the most uncomfortable that either Ifu or Nife had ever experienced. At last, it was their turn. The doctor looked at the results grimly while they studied his face. At last, he looked up at them and said, "I'm afraid I have some very bad news and there is no easy way of breaking it to you. There is a lot of trouble here. Nife your tubes are totally blocked and beaded like that of someone that had long-standing gonorrhea. Ifu you do not have even one life sperm in your semen even though the volume, acidity and every other thing seems alright." He paused.

"Gonorrhea?" Nife exclaimed. "Doctor are you sure of what you are saying? Are these our results? We got married to each other as virgins and have remained faithful to each other…" She trailed off, checked by the fact that there had been no reaction whatsoever from Ifu. She looked at him. Shame, guilt, and something else – was it defeat? – were written all over his face.

She started again. "I'm sure there are other things you want to tell us about, like what we could do next doctor, but we better leave you now. I think my husband and I have a lot that we need to talk over."

The doctor agreed on all counts, and they left.

LESSONS

It is a serious test like this that proves who one's true friends really are. These friends did not have any good intentions at all.

This story was told to illustrate how easy it is to rape a man! Men are much easier to arouse than women. That was why Joseph in The Bible had to run from Portiphar's wife. Unfortunately, when a man is not in full control of himself, he cannot run. That too was what happened to Samson after he drank Delilah's wine.

*Sex is an instinctive need, and **due to** the restrictive training given to children in all cultures, they already have enough sex education to know where the sex organs are located and what they are for. It is not true that such explicit and demonstrative sex education such as Ifu's "friends" planned for him are necessary at all. When they indulged for the first time themselves, who told them what to do?*

The real tragedy of this story was in Ifu's secrecy. If he had bared his heart to his wife that first time, two of them would have taken the full treatment and much damage been prevented. The scar would have been much less than what it turned out to be.

Gonorrhea by its very nature hides in the woman where it stays wreaking untold havoc. It also acts as a reservoir for re-infecting the man. The effect in the man is more easily obvious and so demanding immediate treatment. Promiscuous men act as the disseminators, spreading it from woman to woman.

Gonorrhea is treatable. However, it is every bit as dangerous as the untreatable diseases like HIV-AIDS, Herpes Simplex, and the rest of them.

The situation could have been worse: men have developed many holes around the penis and buttocks area. Men and women have developed blood poisoning, intestinal obstruction, heart diseases and so on. Babies born to mothers with active gonorrhea develop eye infections, meningitis, deafness, and so many other things.

Will Ifu and Nife ever have a baby? Yes, but it would be a costlier and more difficult way to go. The results would also not be as sure as if the event described here never took place (See Index).

VIRTUAL VIRGIN

"*E*ach time I join a couple like this, I feel like going back to my own wedding day all over again. All of you can bear me witness that my beautiful wife will still make a fine bride indeed."

Everybody laughed and clapped. Pastor Vince could be so funny. He and his wife Virginia were indeed beloved in the parish. At their wedding four years before, Virginia had indeed made a beautiful bride. She was the model of a true child of God. There were no rumors of goings on with boys, nor of the lusts of youth attached to her name. All her course mates at the university, and even her lecturers could vouch for her goodness. Her beauty shone from the inside as well as from the outside.

What puzzled everybody was how it was that four years after marriage, Virginia was not yet a mother. People could understand their postponing childbirth for a year or so in order to be "really married". After four years, however, people were really getting puzzled. Was it not Pastor Vince that said it is God's will for people to multiply and increase? Was he not the one that prayed daily for people to receive the power to conceive, and it happened? Should he not also apply the principle of "Physician Heal Thyself" to his case too?

Speculations were rife. Some people said things like "Perhaps God is still creating a special baby for them like an Isaac or a Samuel."

Some others said, "Perhaps the devil has come to take revenge on him for all those people he has been liberating from bondage."

There were even those that said, "Maybe the family planning method they chose in their first year of marriage is over-working."

A very malicious group said things like, "You never know what they did in their youth. All this Holy, Holy attitude we are seeing now may be a cover-up for a terrible past. Nothing can hide forever. Everything one sows sprouts eventually."

Whatever each person's school of thought was, there was no doubt that the continued childlessness of Pastor Vince and his wife had become a real source of concern for the entire congregation. They prayed about it individually for those that were minded to. The elders of the church met and took matters into their own hands. They called a fasting among themselves over the matter. "This has almost become a reproach and we should table it before the Lord and see what he has to say about it."

They did not tell Pastor Vince nor Virginia about their decision until the end of the seven-day program. They then called the couple into the church auditorium together and solemnly told them: "We are confident of your goodness and your zeal in serving the Lord all these years. We are also very concerned that the Lord has not yet blessed you with the fruit of the womb. Rather than go gossiping or speculating about it, we put it to God in prayers. We have lifted you both up to the Lord in prayers over the past seven days and this is what we feel the Lord would have us tell you: YOU MUST GO TO THE HOSPITAL!"

It was a very simple and rather too obvious a conclusion. The elders had other details: Pastor Vince and Virginia were to go to a particular Gynecologist. A special purse was being opened for the treatment. Money had already been pledged into it. More would be added if need be. All the couple had to decide was when to go.

They thanked the elders very much for everything. They promised to go home to think and pray about it. "We will definitely get back to you soon," they promised as they left.

What the elders and the rest of the congregation did not know was that there was A BIG PROBLEM on ground. Pastor Vince had "kept himself" a virgin just as he had preached to others. "Sex is made by God but is meant for marriage only," he had always preached. "Anything that you do with your body outside of marriage is sowing to the devil. Keep yourselves pure until you marry."

That was the Christian standard and he lived by it. He was not hypocritical. The principle had many advantages, and no known disadvantages. So he had thought until he got married himself. To be honest, he had spent a considerable part of the wedding reception trying to keep his mind from wandering at what his first sexual experience would be like. Pastor Vince, after all, had hormones like every other red-blooded young man. Besides, those hormones had been under check for so long.

After the wedding and all the prolonged courtesies that went with it, he was impatient for everyone to go home so that he could be alone with his wife at last. The wife of the District

Superintendent saw the gleam in his eye and interpreted it correctly. She also saw the apprehension in the bride's eyes. She called Pastor Vince aside and counseled him, "You must be patient with your wife. You know these final days of preparing for the wedding has been hectic. She must be very tired from it all. The church has arranged for you to go to the mission holiday Resort from tomorrow. There you will have all the time for two weeks to start marrying. For tonight though, please be patient with her."

A lot was left unsaid. There were several meanings to the communication that had just transpired but Vince understood perfectly what the well-meaning elderly lady was trying to tell him. He resolved that there was no harm in trying anyway. Had he not waited patiently all these years? Was it not now his legal rights, his spiritual rights, his cultural rights, his conjugal rights, in fact his moral obligations to have carnal knowledge of his wife? The advice was good, but advice was not always meant to be taken. He had been polite enough to listen.

But he had reckoned without his bride. Virginia and her bridesmaids were putting away the wedding gifts when Vince entered the guest room allocated to them at the rectory. Noting the pleading look that Virginia gave the other girls, he withdrew again, ostensibly to go and conclude arrangements for their journey the next day. When he came back, the other girls had gone. Virginia had changed out of her wedding gown. That was good, but as soon as Vince himself began to undress, Virginia had shrieked and run into the adjoining toilet and bolted the door from inside. Vince had laughed and thought it all a joke. When he knocked on the door later and found it locked from inside, he became miffed. He rattled the door handle and called out to his wife of a few hours but all he heard were some jumbled sounds. "Come on out Honey," he said in an exaggerated syrupy voice. "This is your husband calling you, wanting you."

The sounds from behind the door became louder. Vince realized that his wife was actually crying and sobbing very hard. That was when Vince became alarmed. He pleaded and cajoled, and finally told her what the wife of the District Superintendent had said. "Come on out," he pleaded soberly, very much unlike the voice he had used before. "Nothing will happen tonight, I promise you. I just want you to rest and sleep for the journey tomorrow."

Virginia came out at last. Vince tried very hard to keep down his disappointment and to restore them to the initial light-heartedness of the day. This was not quite possible. Virginia cleaned her eyes and washed her face. She lay down very rigidly on one side of the bed, as far away as possible from her husband. She kept playing and replaying in her mind all that she knew of what happened between men and women together on a bed. She slept fitfully that night. Anytime Vince brushed against her in his sleep, she would wake up panting like someone that just had a nightmare. At last, it was morning. They left on their honeymoon. The story of that honeymoon could have been told before it happened. There were frustrating moments of trying to copulate. There were incidences of Vince literally chasing Virginia round their room, pleading, cajoling, and even threatening. At one point, out of frustration he tore off her clothes and was going to take her by force, but violence was not really in his nature. The very sight of her weeping, sweating, and trembling in one corner of the room was enough to bring him to his senses. He soothed her, apologized, and helped her to dress up in other clothes. Inside of him, he was confused and utterly frustrated.

There were other couples at the Resort engaged in their own different programs. He thought of seeking counsel from some of them, but everybody seemed to be engaged in their own private programs. They replied to his greetings in such a way that showed they were unwilling to be drawn into any long discussions. At last, he decided that they had better cut short their appointed stay and go back to their base.

This was a very delicate problem. Everybody expected them to be so happy, but it was all a cover-up. Deep inside, Vince was suffering, and Virginia suffered right along for causing him such suffering. They did not know who to turn to. They did not discuss it often between themselves. Among his brothers, it had once slipped out of Vince accidentally. "It's like I'm married, and yet I am not married" he said piteously.

They were all sympathetic and full of advice: "Rape her. Just take her by force. After the first time it becomes easier and she will start yielding to you," said one.

Another one said, "Watch a sexually erotic film with her. That will turn the two of you on and then events could follow from there."

"Why don't you put something in her drink to sedate her and then have sex with her while she's asleep? Bad boys do it all the time" was another suggestion.

"Why don't you just take her to the hospital and ask them to cut her for you" was yet another one.

"I don't know," said the most honest of his brothers. "I've never heard of anyone having such a problem. I have never heard of any such thing in my life. Maybe you should ask the elders what ought to be done in such a situation."

They were all trying to help but Vince was a pastor. He lived by Bible principles which his brothers did not all understand.

He kept the problem to himself for a while not knowing who to tell. He did not want the news to spread like wildfire. He did not go to the elders of his village as one of his brothers had suggested. He finally took it back to the superintendent's wife who had counseled him before. "It's so frustrating Mummy," he said, using the term of respect that was usually applied to such people. "If my contact with her passes the casual holding of hands, she would go all rigid and start sweating profusely. I have taken to sleeping on the couch in the sitting room just so she can get a decent night's sleep. I'm beginning to think that marrying a virgin is a very bad idea indeed."

"Don't talk like that" the superintendent's wife chided him. "Virgins are still the best. I will talk to her and see where the problem is."

She was true to her word. She sent for Virginia and spent hours talking with her. The younger woman seemed to have absolutely nothing to say in her own defense. She kept mute while the superintendent's wife talked and talked, plying her with one advice upon another, and one anecdote after another. When Virginia finally left, she at least left with the resolve to shut her eyes, square her shoulders, and take what was coming to her.

And that was what she literally did. She shut her eyes very tightly, held her body very rigidly while her husband tried to make love to her. It was quite an ordeal. At least, she only twisted herself from side to side. She did not jump off the bed as at other times. Vince did manage to ejaculate at last. Nevertheless, this was not sex as he had envisioned it. He did not cherish repeating the performance often. He did not disturb the superintendent's wife again. He bore it quietly and channeled his energy into other aspects of serving the flock that was in his care until the elders decided to intervene.

The couple indeed went and talked it over like they had promised the elders that they would. They decided that there was nothing to lose. Since the elders had gone to such an extent to even select the doctor and raise the funds, it would be extremely impolite not to go. They should at least have a report to give. They fixed a date with the doctor and arrived there together. It turned out that the doctor was a woman! At least Virginia found that very reassuring. The doctor asked a lot of questions that would have been embarrassing in other settings, but they somehow did not find it so at all. They answered as openly as they could. They admitted that they had attempted to have sex about twice a week during which Vince managed to reach a climax, but which Virginia did not enjoy at all.

She put Virginia on a couch and then exclaimed or so it seemed to them, "Why, you are virtually still a virgin! There is no way to even put in a finger to examine you."

And then the whole story poured out. They told her about the fights, the frustrations, the charade of "playing sex". "I am so surprised she even relaxed enough like this for you to examine her," Vince said with a tinge of bitterness in his voice. "She has never been able to relax like this for me."

The doctor did not need to ask further questions to get the rest of the story. She was very understanding about it too. She went out of her way to reassure them. "It might have to do with a very bad childhood experience that has been buried in your subconscious. Nevertheless, there is nothing that with faith you cannot overcome. God is well-able. It will take time and patience, but we will get there eventually."

She fixed time to see them individually, and sometimes together. She counseled Vince to be patient with his wife. "Talk with her often. Communication is to a woman probably what sex is to a man. Win her confidence. Let her know that her greatest value to you is not just as a sex-piece. Vince wondered if he had not been doing so all along. However, as they talked, he found out he could really improve, and he did so very willingly. It was all in the attitude.

To Virginia she counseled that she must stop seeing her husband as the enemy, and sex as a punishment. "It was made by God after all. He has made all things for us to enjoy bounteously and thankfully."

Together she had them play what they called silly roles in her consulting room. Many times, they had to make what they called amusing conversations. Sometimes she made Virginia undress before her husband and vice versa. Sometimes she was there to guide them. Some other times she gave them instructions on what to do and busied herself at another part of the hospital. It took many sessions, spread over about six months. Sometimes it looked as if they were regressing rather than progressing. On some days they virtually held prayer meetings with the doctor.

But the day finally came when ***Virginia actually invited her husband to come and make love!*** This was the final turning point. He could not believe his ears. He was very hesitant at first but hey! This was what he had been longing for all along. There was a bit of the old rigidity as he penetrated for that first time, but it did not last for long. She relaxed and actually began to enjoy it. As the doctor had told them, the power to enjoy sex or not was really "in the mind."

It must have been that first "proper sex" that resulted in the conception of their first baby. "Christian" they named him, in honor of the sweet and supportive fellowship of the brethren.

Today, Christian has three other siblings, but out of that ordeal, his parents got more than babies. They have developed a ministry of helping other people with sexual difficulties in marriage. Because they went through it firsthand, their own counsel has a greater power. It is also much more effective than those of other people in the same line of counseling.

APPEARANCES

This story may seem preposterous, but it is so common. Many people that others are pitying and agonizing over because of their childlessness are either not having sex at all, or not having it satisfactorily.

Someone once said that so much time is spent teaching the girl-child to be sexually chaste that when she grows into an adult woman a lot more time has to be spent teaching her to be sexually yielded to her husband.

Another person also said that whereas most men see sex as a means of Recreation, most women see it as a mode of Procreation! Sex was made by God for both recreation and procreation but within the boundaries of marriage. Forget what else modernism has to say.

The greatest organ of sex is the mind. A mind that is attuned to enjoy sex would definitely enjoy it. Sexual problems among women are very common ranging from never enjoying sex to enjoying it only sometimes. Fortunately, it is only a few women that will come out with the kind of extreme problems that Virginia had. Even these would vary from a mildly contained desire to run to out-rightly fighting and sometimes dangerously wounding the man.

The root-cause is not always easy to pin-point. It might be a deeply buried unpleasant sexual experience in childhood, undergone by the individual, or even just merely witnessed. Under hypnosis, a patient undergoing treatment for this sort of problem reported having seen her parents having sex as a very young child. She thought then that her father was trying to kill her mother!

Most times however, it's just a psychological conditioning that the society puts on everybody in order to inculcate the dangers of pre-marital sex. This gets absorbed and over-synthesized by some individuals more than others. It has to do with personality types also.

Definitive treatment therefore must involve psychological re-conditioning. Many people are not willing to wait this out. They declare prematurely that it does not work. The dangers of this is that they pass on their fear of sex to their daughters – biological, fostered, and mentored.

For those that persist with treatment there is usually a total cure. They go on to have many productive sexual years with no relapse.

TWO TO TANGO

*I*t was a high society wedding, attended by all the Who is who in the business and the political world. Money was not spared. Everything was done or provided for to excess. The marriage of Obong and Uduak was high society meeting with and merging with itself. It was momentous. It was a real event!

The groom was a businessman based in the United States. He had other interests in several other countries, but he never forgot his home. Wherever he was, he always wended home "To touch base!" His father was a first-class traditional chief who had many important political connections at the grassroots, state, and Federal levels. The bride was a modest home-grown girl but her father moved with the political bigwigs. In the right circles, he was discreetly known as "The Kingmaker". She was still an undergraduate but was classed among the "Special students". She had lodgings off-campus. She had her very own car to make moving around easy. The marriage was really arranged to the interests of both fathers, but Uduak and Obong had met, liked each other and as the common saying went "hit it off immediately!"

Despite all appearances, Uduak was still the modest and home-grown girl she portended to be. She had had her own fair share of experimenting with sex while still in secondary school. In the University, she did not need to "desperately live it up" as other girls were doing despite the campaigns against HIV-AIDS. She was studying for a degree in political science just for the joy of it. She was not hoping to make a career of it unlike her course mates. She did not need to earn a living. However, as her father pointed out, "You never know what can crop up in future." She came from money, and was marrying into money, but idleness never did anyone any atom of good. Besides, in the circles in which they moved it was useful to talk about "My days at the University…" Her father had also assured her that going to university was a great way of making contacts and staying in touch with the grassroots.

The wedding was satisfactorily lavish. The honeymoon was to be at The Bahamas. Everything had already been processed and paid for. It was a wedding gift from one of the groom's business associates. The bride had no objections. Immediately after the wedding reception though, they were to stay overnight at the Port-Harcourt Sheraton and leave the following day.

Uduak looked forward to her wedding night with mixed feelings. They had made a pact of "No sex before marriage" as a mark of respect to both their parents. It was also so as not to provide gossip fodder for the ever-hungry media. They had succeeded too, against all odds. That night at Port-Harcourt was to be their first night together.

Uduak's things had been packed away into her new home. The next morning, a driver was to take their traveling effects to the airport. They had come to the airport with only their over-night bags. Uduak wondered how that first time would be: should they undress together and then fall into bed? Should they fall into bed and then undress each other like in the movies? More romantically, would they be too hungry for each other that they would not even bother to undress?

At the end, none of those things happened. As soon as they were checked into their hotel room, Obong told her to start unpacking. He needed to see off the friends that had brought them. He also had to see to one or two business concerns. "I'll be right back," he said.

Uduak thought that "right back" would be in about ten minutes or less. There was not much to unpack. They did not need anything. The hotel provided all that. She duly got out their changes of clothes and hung them in the wardrobe. She laid out the things they would need the following morning before going to the airport. She slowly went through the comforts the hotel was offering them, and yet Obong did not return.

She decided to undress and take a long bath. Perhaps he would come back, see her there, find her seductive and join her. That would be another romantic flavor to add to the Honeymoon Tales she would regale friends with afterwards.

In the Sheraton, one could bathe ten times over without denting their water or towel supplies. Uduak lingered in the bathroom till she began to feel drowsy. By the time she emerged she was surprised to see that it was already past ten. Obong had still not returned. She began to feel the injustice of it all. Should business not have given way to pleasure tonight of all nights? It was not every day that one got married! But she was a new bride, and she was not going to let anything steal The Mood from her. She wore her specially chosen seductive nightgown and arranged herself on the bed the best way she knew how. "Ah well," she reasoned, "The varieties will only add to the telling of the stories."

She flipped through the newspapers and magazines by the bedside and found nothing interesting. She switched on the television and surfed the available channels. Nothing interested her. At last she settled on a re-run of old love ballads. The toll of the excitement of the day, the effect of the long bath, and the soothing melodies finally all lulled her to sleep. One singer was soulfully crooning, "I love you babeee…"

Perhaps it was the sinking of the bed, or the alcohol fumes that woke Uduak. She woke up to find that Obong was just getting into bed. She looked at the bedside clock and discovered that it was two o'clock in the morning. He stank like a brewery. She had not even known that he drank. In all their period of courtship, he had portended to be a teetotaler.

"I waited for you" she said drowsily.

"Sorry, I was with the boys," Obong slurred. He fell instantly asleep, still fully clothed.

Uduak was rather glad that there was to be no love-making that night. She just rolled over, subconsciously moving as far away as possible from her stinking husband. The next day she woke bright and early and really took a good look at him. He was worse by the harsh daylight. He looked much older than his thirty-three years. He had lines of dissipation all over his face. With a slack jaw and rivulets of saliva trailing down the corner of his mouth, he looked revolting. His snore was not attractive either. She wondered what she had got herself into. She wondered briefly whether to confront him about coming in late the previous night but decided against it. "I will not be the nagging wife" she resolved in her heart firmly. I will put in my best to make this marriage work." She did not know then how much would be required of her, but that resolve helped a lot!

The flight to The Bahamas was uneventful. Obong was being the perfectly attentive "Dream Husband". He had apologized for coming in late. "I was just so carried away by knowing that I would not be seeing them for a long time. I allowed myself to indulge."

"Didn't you say that you gave up drinking some years ago?" Uduak asked in a voice that she hoped was non-complaining.

"I did," Obong answered "but this was like a special occasion. It was a going away event."

They had smiled at each other and got on with the other serious business of getting ready to go.

Their hotel accommodation at The Bahamas was no less opulent than the one at Port-Harcourt. This time however, they were quartered in what the hotel called a self-contained cottage. They donned their swimming attires and joined the rest of the world that was seeking a tan even though they did not need any themselves.

Their cottage entitled them to a secluded bit of the beach, but they were never alone. Obong was forever wanting to be with other people. "It's good for making business contacts," he explained. "You never know when such casual acquaintances will come in useful."

Obong had not become drunk again, but they had not yet made love. The first day that they arrived, he pronounced both of them very tired from the journey. By the next day he had recovered sufficiently to play vigorous beach football with a group of American teenagers that they met at the beach. That night he had been too exhausted to even eat supper. The next day, he had taken Uduak dancing right after lunch. They had eaten supper at a quaint restaurant by the beach and joined in the native samba celebration till the small hours of the morning. The following day, he had agreed to go on a three-day excursion into the hinterlands with two Canadian families.

"When are we going to be alone by ourselves?" Uduak protested. "I thought that the idea of a honeymoon is for us to get to be by ourselves and know ourselves better!"

"I know, Honey, I know" he answered. "It will not always be like this. There are many other holidays that we will go on together."

"Exactly!" she agreed "So let us make this one special. We will never be newly-weds again. On those other holidays we can make the business contacts."

"Okay," Obong agreed surprising her. "Since we already have these appointments, let us keep them. Afterwards we shall change to a new pace."

But the pace did not change at all. It became more hectic if anything. Always, it involved other people. With less than a week to the end of their holiday, she decided to change tactics. They had gone to bed exhausted the previous day. Waking up first as usual the next morning, she had gone and showered and then come back to begin to undress her still-sleeping husband.

"What are you doing?" he shouted startled awake.

"Undressing my husband for sex," she replied undaunted, and with a provocative smile. "We have been married for almost two weeks now and we are yet to make love. I thought sex was a vital part of all this commotion about marriage and honeymoon. Every day is so packed full of activities when we should be so much together in bed having sex. Everybody will understand."

Obong swung his feet out of bed. He sat at the edge, supporting his head with his hands. Uduak continued to knead his back and shoulder, hugging him from behind even as she talked.

"Oh!" he groaned over and over but not in sexual ecstasy. Uduak did not know how to interpret this. Was it dismay, regret, or what? Suddenly he jumped up from the bed and went into the bathroom. She stretched out invitingly on the bed to await his return. "Today," she resolved in her heart, "we arc going to consummate this marriage!"

Obong stayed for long in the bathroom. She heard water running, then the toilet flushing. She heard him brushing his teeth. And then he was shaving with the electric razor. After that there was a long pause during which she heard nothing. At last, he came out. He looked at her for a long time lying there on the bed in her birthday suit. He brought a chair close to the bed. Before he sat, he took a bed sheet and covered up her nakedness. And then he said in a curiously serious voice, "We need to talk."

Uduak suddenly felt very cold with apprehension. However, having resolved to get to the bottom of the matter, she waited. She sat up against the headboard and tucked the sheet around her. They had promised to meet with another couple for breakfast, but she was not going anywhere. She decided they had to resolve this first.

Obong did most of the talking, Uduak asked a question from time to time. The whole story then emerged. The essence of it was that Obong had been discovered to be diabetic when he was just sixteen years old. He was put on daily insulin injections and told that if he adopted a moderate lifestyle, he could still do all that his mates could. With the rebellion of adolescence, Obong had decided that any life not lived to the fullest was not worth living at all. He had smoked, drank, and partied very hard with the hardest of the pack. He had even dabbled into recreational drugs. He hardly ever remembered to take his daily injections.

"This went on for about seven years until I collapsed one day. At first my friends thought that it was just a bad hangover. When I remained unconscious for two whole days they panicked and took me to the hospital. That was when it was discovered that I had developed terrible complications of diabetes. I was just twenty-five years, but I had hypertension, some damage to my eyes, my kidneys, and even some nerves. It was like a death sentence. I had lived a hard and foolish life. The doctors were good and encouraging. They said that a lifestyle change would help a lot. I was willing to change then. Some of the damages could be reversed, some could halt but some were permanent, and irreversible.

"I quit drinking, smoking, and doing drugs. When I was about to marry, I told my doctor that I could hardly achieve erections. He told me that it was probably due to some of the medications I had to take for hypertension. He changed it and matters improved. But then my blood pressure started rising and I had to go back on the medications. We are still juggling to find out what is good for me – another medication or reduced dosages of the same medication." He took a deep breath. "I have been deliberately postponing making love to you. I don't know whether I can get it up or not."

Uduak stared at him wide-eyed as he finished up. At last, she said "You have not even tried with me at all".

"I am afraid to try" he answered sadly.

"But you would want to have children." It was a statement, not a question.

"Very much! Very, very much" Obong intoned.

"Then I think we can work out something. My father always says that where there is a will, there is a way."

They did try to have sex. They even managed to work something out. When Uduak returned from the Bahamas she had so many tales to tell about her perfectly romantic and amorous honeymoon. The pictures were so beautiful. The other girls could only envy her. What more, she was always flying off to one place or the other for a holiday with her wonderfully attentive husband. When two years after the marriage they had not had a baby yet, she told everybody to grow up and be modern. She had school to finish, national service to do, and social events to grace. How could a baby fit into this kind of tight schedule?

School was soon over, and then Youth Service. After that they went abroad more frequently. At a stage Uduak settled there to live while Obong continued shuttling. She did not "Touch base" again for five years. When she did, she came with three children – a four-year old son, another two-year old son, and a brand-new baby girl. They all looked very plump and charming.

"You seem to be having your babies in quick succession," one of her friends told her. "How many are you planning to have altogether?"

"I think my child-bearing days are over," Uduak replied flippantly. One can never say. "I think I am ready to face a new phase of my life now. I will raise these ones while I pursue my career and try to re-enter the political world. I can see that a lot has happened in this country in my absence. I plan to be a part of the new face of this country."

She has been too.

DANCING

Unlike the previous story, the problem here is with the man. Whereas female orgasm is not necessary for conception to take place, male orgasm is.

Many people take it for granted that most men always want to have sex. The truth is that most men that behave "Macho" really cannot perform sexually. They are just trying to cover up. Research has shown that there is a great reduction in sperm count in men universally. This is also true about their sexual drives. Speculations on what is responsible for this have ranged from increased stress of work; junk dieting; increased radio-active emissions, environmental pollutants, depleting ozone layer etcetera.

The commonest cause of erectile problems in men though is anxiety and depression. Next to it is alcohol and substance abuse. Diabetes comes a close third. In fact, the first sign of diabetes in a man could be inability to achieve erections. Medications, like some anti-hypertensives, sedatives, and anti-psychotics also cause erectile dysfunction. Some of these diseases manifest with age. Increasing age itself also comes with loss of libido. Feeling unfairly compared with other people worsens the problem. So does feeling under pressure to "perform".

Most men improve spontaneously, without treatment when they understand what is happening to them. Slowing down at work, learning how to relax, stopping substance abuse, and so on also improve matters. Many damages begin to reverse. Unfortunately, some of it is permanent.

So, were those children really Uduak and Obong's?

Probably. By juggling Obong's medications, making use of modern knowledge in treatment of infertility (See the index), by having a very understanding wife, and enough money, these things are possible. The fact that the babies were born in quick succession bears this out. This was also wise because with age, the existing problems become worse. Other complications might also develop.

SHOOTING BLANKS

"*Y*ou should go and check yourself," Ike shouted at Nkoli. "There is nothing wrong with me at all. I already have three children. Three! You are the one who cannot make babies."

Nkoli shut up as she had done in times past. She just retreated to one corner to weep hot and bitter tears. She had been warned by her friends and relatives not to marry Ike but she had felt that at thirty, age was not on her side. Ike had been so courteous and attentive. He was unlike so many young men that she knew. What else could one possibly want in a marriage?

Ike, on his part was really only looking for someone to help him care for his children. They were aged eighteen months to thirty months. He had felt that Nkoli would be desperate enough to yield without all the expensive courtship required by young ladies these days. His role had come to him easily. He knew what he wanted, and he acted his part in order to get it. He had been proven right – again!

Ike was not a widower. His former wife Adaku had left after almost ten years of marriage. "Left" was not the exact term. She had been driven away by his relatives. For the first five years of their marriage, they had no baby. Adaku had gone for all the tests required by the hospital and never troubled him to come along. Suddenly, after the five years of testing, she had suddenly become pregnant. After the first baby, it was as if a

floodgate had been opened. She had three babies in quick
succession so that the gaps between them was like a year each.
One day, Adaku was caught red-handed in the act of adultery
with one of Ike's near-kinsmen. The kinsman had been
cautioned and disciplined but Ike's brothers had given Adaku a
thorough beating. His womenfolk had come and escorted her
back to her father's house in disgrace, as was the custom of the
land. This method meant that they wanted no reconciliation
with her, ever.

Adaku was not allowed to go with her children.
Children were supposed to belong to the husband. In disgrace,
she was not even allowed to come to see them, nor to contact
them in any way. If they grew up and decided to go to see her,
well and good. They were never to bring her back to their
family compound again.

That was how Ike found himself a single parent of three
toddlers. The people that had got rid of his wife did not ask
how he was going to cope. They all had their own families to
run. They were convinced that they had performed their civic
duties in helping him get rid of the evil that was breeding in his
house. He was supposed be a man and solve the rest of his
problem by himself. That was what he did in finding Nkoli to
come to care for his children.

Nkoli's mother had wept and pleaded with her when
she announced that she was going to marry Ike. "That family is
trouble," she said. "Anyone marrying into it is asking for
trouble."

But Nkoli was adamant. It was not as if suitors were
falling over themselves to marry her. She was not that
beautiful. All she had was a reasonable education and a steady

income. She was not under any illusions about it at all. She was not getting any younger. All her friends were married. Even her two younger sisters were married. She wanted to be seen as a married woman too.

"You will be a stepmother," her best friend told her. "No matter how good you are with the children, the neighbors and their relatives will always remind them that you are not their real mother. When they are growing up they will deal with you. They will think you were the reason their mother was driven out of the house. When they are fully grown, they will want to bring back their mother. Where will that leave you then?"

Even with such a factual and gloomy picture Nkoli still refused to be dissuaded. She was going to marry Ike, not his children. It was true they came as part of the package, but Ike was the main thing. From what she had seen of him before marriage, he was very courteous and considerate. Surely, that would more than make up for any other flaws in the marriage, his children, and his other relatives. And so Nkoli married him.

The honeymoon period, such as it was, was very short-lived. Nkoli soon saw that she had married the proverbial python who when the borrowed parts were returned was revealed as the slimy cruel creature it really was. She soon discovered that all Ike really wanted was an unpaid nanny for his children. A nanny who would sometimes grace his bed as a favor; and bring in some money for him besides. Nkoli lived in misery. She dared not share her problems with anyone. She dreaded being told "I told you so…" Nkoli bore patiently with her afflictions and counted her blessings. At least she was out of the marriage market. If only she could get pregnant and have a baby of her own, she would count herself contented despite all the prevailing circumstances.

But Nkoli did not get pregnant. A few months into the marriage she went to see a doctor about this. The doctor reassured her that pregnancy did not happen as quickly nor as automatically as people assumed. She had to have been trying for at least a year without succeeding before even thinking of whether there was a problem or not.

A year passed. Nkoli endured lovemaking with Ike because she was hoping to be rewarded by a pregnancy, but it did not happen. She went back to the doctor and was subjected to so many tests. Some of these did not come cheap but the results all showed that there was no reason why she should not have a baby. "Just be patient" the doctor told her, "It takes more time for some people than for others. We have to test your husband too to be sure there is nothing wrong from that aspect as well."

That was how Nkoli bore the message back to Ike. Ike exploded out of all proportions. "Did I send you for the tests?" he raved. "It comes from having independent money of your own. If you were looking for what to spend money on you should have told me. I would have given you a list of things that needs doing. Take this leaking roof for instance…" He went on and on until Nkoli was weary. She left him alone just to shut off the flow.

A few months passed with Nkoli still waiting patiently as the doctors had instructed. One of her colleagues at work suggested that the problem might be from Ike. Courageously, Nkoli went back to persuade him to do the test. "There is nothing wrong with me," he exploded again, very predictably.

"I could not have had these three children if there was anything wrong with me. The problem must be from you. Show me any child you have had anywhere. Do you think that the fact that you menstruate every month proves that you are fertile? You must be the barren one of the two of us. Check it: you have a maternal aunt that died childless recently. Your father's elder sister has been married for thirty years now. What does she have to show for it? Don't let me mention several of your cousins on both your father's and your mother's side…"

Nkoli went out of the room in tears. Four years passed and she still did not get pregnant. By now she was thirty-five years. She was more desperate than ever. She decided to try a different doctor. This doctor subjected her to all the tests she had done before. He still found nothing wrong with her. He also suggested that her husband had better come and be tested too. "Oh No! No!" Nkoli said rather too quickly. "There is nothing wrong with him. He already has three children from his former wife. He is able to achieve an erection at the drop of a pin. His sexual performance is certainly above scrutiny. Besides, no member of his family is barren. The fault must be all mine."

This particular doctor was even more skeptical than the last one. He asked her several questions about her husband that she had no answers for: Did he have mumps as a child or any other serious childhood diseases? Had he had any operation on his scrotum or groin? Nkoli knew that he had operation scars in both groins but being ignorant of such matters had always assumed that they were for appendicitis. The doctor's questions made her wonder. Aloud she asked, "Is it possible for him not to be able to have children after the first three?"

"Anything is possible" affirmed the doctor and then went into technical details about things that had to do with aging, anti-sperm antibodies, subsequent blockage of the tubes and so on and so forth. Nkoli did not understand it all but she did understand that the problem may not all be from her alone after all.

She went home. This time she did not confront her husband but decided to tackle his mother instead. Even that, she did in an oblique manner. "Uzo seems to be limping on his left leg. I think he is just trying to imitate his father and be the guy." Uzo was her stepson.

Mama loved telling stories. She told Nkoli about how Ike had been very grievously sick as a child. They had to be admitted for a long time in the hospital at the big city. "They said it was a type of blood cancer, and gave him all manner of treatment. We thought he would die. Even the doctors tried to tell us that he might not live to become an adult but here he is now! He is fully grown and a father himself. All he has left over from that terrible time is that slight limp. That shows you that doctors do not know it all."

"Indeed!" Nkoli agreed meditatively, and then asked, "Was that when he also had the operation in his groins?"

"Hmm, that was about two years earlier and it was another story altogether." Mama launched into another saga of how Ike was always suffering from hernia as a child. She pronounced it *"Hei-nia"*. "At first, they taught us how to correct it if it pained him too much. At a stage it became difficult to correct. He had to be operated, first on the right side, and later on the left side. As if that was not enough, soon after the operation there was an epidemic of mumps. Other children had mumps and quickly recovered but not Ike. The sickness seemed to settle at the place of the *hei-nia* operation. The place was so red and so swollen. At a stage it even began to bring out pus. Ike would cry piteously in pain. day and night. We spent two weeks in the hospital at that time, but he eventually recovered fully. There is no doubt about it, this husband of yours is truly a survivor. I think God just meant him to live and not die."

Unwittingly, Mama had provided all the answers that the doctor sought. The news did not look good at all. Nkoli began to see that the problem might not be from her at all. But Ike had fathered three children before she came along.

Nkoli did not know who to talk all this over with. Her mother had also been waiting as anxiously for Nkoli's babies to start coming. With her mother-in-law's revelations fresh on her mind therefore, she told her mother about all that the doctor had asked and how Mama had answered them. Nkoli's mother linked it all together to other events in the past and asked her daughter "Didn't they say that Ike's first wife also stayed five years before having her first baby?"

"Yes," reiterated Nkoli. "That was why I was hoping that my own period of waiting would also soon be over."

But that was not what was on her mother's mind. "Didn't everyone also know that Adaku was caught in adultery and was disgraced? Use your head Girl, read in between the lines. Adaku must have come to the same conclusions you are coming to now and decided to help herself out."

Light dawned on Nkoli. The story was altogether too plausible. Adaku was a traditionalist and would have had no qualms about going outside to get the pregnancy, provided the baby was born in her husband's house. The fact that she was caught with Ike's kinsman was also a consolidating point. A kind person would have wanted to keep it all within the family. Nkoli decided that it was about time that she confronted Ike with it all.

In the meantime, Ike's mother mentioned her conversation with Nkoli to her son. "She was so curious about your childhood illnesses and so I told her. I did not tell her that the doctors had also mentioned that you might never father a baby. I had told Adaku the same stories and she was wise and found her way. Be nice to this girl. She will stay with you too if you treat her well."

Light also dawned on Ike. He had known all the stories about his childhood illnesses but had never heard the one of never being able to father a child. The very next day, he took himself to a medical laboratory in town and posing under a different name had the test done. The result came out: he was producing semen alright but there was no single live sperm in it!

Three days later he went to repeat it at another laboratory. They got exactly the same result. He had a friend that worked at the hospital. He arranged to have it done about a week after he did the first one. He told the friend that the specimen was for another friend of his who was too shy to come himself. He received all the instruction about what "The Friend" was to do. When he came to collect the results, his friend flippantly said, "tell that friend of yours that he is shooting blanks. This sperm will never be able to impregnate any woman. He should beg another man to do it for him." And then he laughed very heartily at his own joke.

Ike saw red. How could a man joke about another man's life like that? He went home seething inside. It was that same evening that Nkoli decided to confront him. Anxiety had made her voice shrill and higher than usual. "Do the tests" she said. "If you say there is nothing wrong with you, then prove it by doing the tests. What are you afraid they might find?"

That was when Ike started to beat his wife! He had so many vices, but beating women had never been one of them. That day however, he was tired and very angry. He had just received confirmation that he was less than the man that he thought he was. Someone he had always considered a very good friend had made fun of him. The children that he had always thought were his, werc not! Hc let lose all this pent-up anger on Nkoli. He battered her till she was unconscious. Maybe he would even have killed her but for the intervention of his mother and some neighbors. Nkoli was taken to the hospital for treatment. From there, she returned to her father's house. Ike made no attempt to come to apologize. That was alright with her people. They returned the dowry that had been paid on her head. This was a traditional way of saying that as far as they were concerned, the marriage was over. "We gave her to you to marry, not to kill" they said.

Ike never remarried. From that day, the monster in him emerged. He began to drink heavily and to live dangerously. He seemed to have a death wish. He neglected his children badly. They would have run wild but for the care of his mother, their grandmother.

Nkoli, on her part, would have been content to live out her days in her father's house. However, on the eve of her thirty-eighth birthday, an old bachelor in her office proposed to her. He was fifteen years older than her. Her friends teased her mercilessly about that. He was the exact opposite of Ike in almost everything. They got married, not really hoping for children. Nkoli became pregnant almost immediately. She delivered a set of twins by operation. Less than two years later, she had a repeat operation to deliver her second set of twins. After that she decided to plan her family by starting on contraceptives.

Their home is rather quiet despite the sets of twins, but it is also a very happy home.

SHOOTING

It is not every man that produces semen that has live sperms in them. It is also not true that a man that had children in the past can always have more in the future.

Rarely do all the childhood diseases described here happen to any one person. This story was written to show that childhood illnesses in boys as well as in girls should be taken very seriously. Mumps, malnutrition, and a few other diseases are especially implicated. If a boy is always touching his private parts, the parents should not only just scold him and tell him how indecent this is. They should also find out if he is touching it because it is painful, itchy or feels funny. If it is any of these, treatment should be sought as soon as possible, from suitably qualified personnel.

When the area shows redness or swelling, it is even more ominous. A hernia should be taken care of at once except if a doctor advises otherwise, perhaps until the child is a bit older.

Even in adolescence and early adulthood, some diseases still affect sperm production: liver disease, cancers, working with radiation, jobs like welding, long-distance driving, wearing hot and tight clothing etcetera can affect sperm production (See index). Some men for some unknown reason also begin to produce antibodies to their own sperms at some point in life. The trigger for this is not known and therefore it cannot be prevented. The lesson is for men to also try to complete their families as early in life as possible. A colleague once said that "Just as women carry expiry dates, men also have a label of 'Best Before…'"

Treatment of infertility due to male factor is notoriously difficult but still possible (See index). This is still one case in which prevention is infinitely better than cure.

STRESS AND DISTRESS

"*N*o matter what you do, don't let Keme know the true situation of things. She will just worry herself to death."

This was what everyone said. Keme's basic fabric worried a lot about everything, but she would always be the first to deny it. "I'm not worried at all. I am just concerned" she would say.

Perhaps that was just different ways of saying the same thing. It was really her caring nature that attracted Onoja to her in the first instance. Keme came from a comfortable background and had a well-paid job. However, she was perpetually in want because she had a very generous nature. She would give away all she had, even to her own inconvenience.

Onoja, on the other hand, had a more cautious nature, even though he was not tight-fisted either. His more organized life balanced Keme's own. They were two very pleasant people. Their families approved of the match. "It will be interesting" they said, "to see what their children would turn out to be: like Keme, like Onoja, like both, or like neither!"

But a year after the wedding, there was still no sign of pregnancy though they both desired it. Typically, Keme worried about it. She went to the hospital and dragged Onoja along with her. They were subjected to the endless questions and embarrassing physical examinations. Keme made sure that they both did all the required tests. Finally, they were told, "You are both fine. "There is no reason why you should not have a baby together. I will just prescribe some medications to give your systems a push and remind them of their duties."

The medications were simple to take though. The side-effects were more difficult to bear. The corresponding instructions on habits to adopt, and the timing of sexual intercourse were easy enough to follow. The couple waited patiently like the doctor told them to and yet nothing happened. Eighteen months into their marriage, Keme found them another doctor based on the advice of one of her friends. "It never hurts to try" she said to her husband trying to convince him. "After all, there is safety in a multitude of counsel."

Onoja felt that they had not yet worn out the patience of the former doctor, but he was finally worn down by his wife's persistence. Just for the sake of his own peace of mind he went along with her. This second doctor began all the questions and examinations and tests afresh. He still came to exactly the same conclusion after it all. "You are two perfectly healthy people. There is no reason why you should not make a bay together."

He did suggest some modern techniques of overcoming such "Unexplained infertility". "We could artificially inseminate Keme with Onoja's sperms. There is no monkey business about that" he assured them. "Both of you will be there and be awake and follow all the processes as we do them. It is like giving the sperms a leg up in their journey of going to fertilize the egg. It will overcome any minor difficulties that we have not taken note of."

Keme and Onoja discussed it at length. At last, they decided to give it a trial anyway. It was cheap enough. For three consecutive months they tried this. It just did not click for them, as the doctor put it. "Maybe I was just never meant to be a mother" Keme wailed.

"Don't be silly" Onoja chided her playfully. "All the doctors said that we should just be patient. Can't you stretch it a bit more?"

Keme was not amused. "Maybe we were not meant to marry each other" she fretted to her best friend Kate. "Maybe if he were married to another woman, and I to another man, we would have been making babies."

"Don't be an idiot!" Kate told her. However, she proceeded to regale her with tales of people in whom that sort of thing happened. Keme's anxiety was fed to over-bloating.

Every month her period came as regularly as clockwork. This would throw her into moderately deep depression. She faithfully observed all the doctors told her about her maximum fertility period. She dutifully marked the dates on a calendar and tried to get her husband to make love to her on the right days. Poor Onoja tried to comply most times. Some other times he was very genuinely tired from work. Once he told her off very sharply. "This is having sex according to the books! I find sex totally unenjoyable when it cannot be spontaneous and playful".

This only added to what Keme had to worry about. She complained to her mother, "And now, I don't even have my husband's support."

"Don't be silly" her mother rebuked her. "You know that Onoja loves you very much. Such good men are difficult to find these days."

"African men don't see love that way," Keme persisted gloomily. "If there is no child in this marriage people will soon start encouraging him to have an affair and at least produce an heir. You know that his entire family, and maybe even some of you will support him then."

There was no pacifying Keme once she began worrying like this. With the breeding of a lifetime, her mother just smoothly changed the topic.

"You worry about it a lot" Mercy and Mike told her. They were very good old friends of hers who had also been through a long period of infertility. By then, had babies of their own. "Try to stop worrying about it. Focus on something else. You know that we are saying this from experience."

"Worry? Worry" I am not worried about it at all. It's just that…that…" and she started crying. She sobbed uncontrollably. Her friends could see for themselves that what her lips were saying was not what her heart believed at all.

Come to think about it, how could one not worry about what bothered one most? Maybe any other person could, but not Keme. They consoled her and commiserated with her. Little did they know that their counsel to focus on another thing would be taken sooner than later. It happened in a most unexpected way.

One day Keme got to her well-paid job to find out that the place was still locked. Her co-workers that had got to work before her were standing around outside. "What is it?" Keme asked. "What is happening?"

"Just go to the notice board and see for yourself" someone advised her.

The notice board was just outside the main entrance. Keme went there to see for herself. She moved into the strangely quiet group already clustered there. "Stunned" did not begin to describe the general feeling of the workers. Overnight, their offices were closed. The bank was taking over the premises because of some long-standing debts. The workers had not been given any notice whatsoever. They were not even allowed in to collect any of their personal effects. Some of them claimed to have left some valuables at their desks. All their pleas fell on deaf ears. The members of their management were nowhere to be seen. The strange security guards glared at them malevolently, as if ready for any trouble they might foment.

On an impulse, Keme decided to call her husband. She needed to hear his voice. She did not want to go back to their empty house and face the depression alone till he returned in the evening. She dialed his office and waited while they called him. "Thank God you called" he began even before she had the chance to say anything. "I was just thinking of driving over to your office now. Your mother called after you left. She said your father had a stroke two days ago. The doctors say that his condition is bad."

The scream that escaped from Keme was ear-piercing. The people at Onoja's office started scolding him for breaking such news to his wife in that manner. "Women are delicate creatures" they said. "You must study how to break such news to them!"

"That's telling me," Onoja said to himself. "Women are delicate in such ways. My wife is even more so." He silently chided himself on such foolishness. However, there was really no easy way of saying it. Immediate decisions needed to be made. In the event it aided his getting permission to go off for the rest of the day so that he could take care of his wife. He had to organize for her to leave for the village.

When he reached Keme's office, he took in the situation. He began to understand the double blow that his wife had received in the space of what was really a few short minutes. Being a very practical person though, he looked around, found her and took her home to comfort her. He helped her to pack a few things and saw her off to the motor park on the way to the village. "Perhaps," he reasoned to himself, "the change of scene and having to care for her father will somehow relieve her anxieties. To her he said, "Please greet everybody for me. I shall definitely be around by the weekend to see how he is getting on."

Money was scarce then and promised to be scarcer in the near future with Keme out of work. He managed to scrape enough together for her to contribute towards her father's treatment. This cheered her up a bit.

Keme's father had been unconscious the whole week but late in the afternoon on Friday he suddenly opened his eyes. He was even very lucid. Onoja waked in just as everyone was exclaiming over this wonder. They all had a very wonderful re-union. There was a lot of hope that Papa's situation had turned the bend as they say. Everyone hoped that from then on he would be on the mend. They laughed, and they cried tears of happiness.

Onoja had gone with some rather bad news that he had been wondering whether to share with Keme or not. He wondered how to go about it if he chose to do so. Buoyed by Papa's miraculous recovery, he decided that he would take the bull by the horn and tell her anyway. Papa's room became too noisy. The nurse came to order everybody out. He took Keme to a park bench in the hospital garden. "We may be making major changes when you return" he began. "The Landlord came to increase our rent. At work, I am being asked to go to a town four hundred kilometers away. They are giving me a choice: if I go, my salary shall remain the same. If I stay, it will be at a reduced salary. There are also the chances that I might soon be declared redundant and retrenched, anyway."

Keme listened quietly. She tried to take it all in. Even as she pondered it, somebody ran towards them. "Come! Come quickly! Papa's condition has changed again. He is breathing with difficulty. The doctors and nurses are working on him right now. They have ordered all of us out of the room, even Mama!"

Everybody knew that this could mean only one thing: Papa was dying. Thirty minutes later, a nurse came out to confirm it to the gathered family. Papa was indeed dead!

Keme did not scream. The grief was too deep for a scream. She felt so overwhelmed. The whole world was collapsing around her: her job; Onoja's job; their house that they had lived in for so many years, and now her father! She clung to her husband dry-eyed. It was only the strength of her grip that betrayed the depth of her grief.

Onoja was deeply moved too. He knew that his first duty was to comfort his wife. He simply held her. He told her over and over, "It's okay. It's okay to cry. It's okay to be sad." He hardly knew what else to say.

He led her to the car and took her home. Others went about the other numerous errands concerning the appropriate disposal of the dead. Entwined in sorrow like this, it was inevitable that they should make love. It was slow, languorous love, free of any expectation, and free of any calculations. It was just two people trying to find comfort and solace in each other.

Papa was buried. People lingered for some time in order to comfort Mama. Eventually they began to leave. Keme and Onoja had to get back to town to solve their job and accommodation problems. In view of how tight their budget was going to be without Keme's added income; and in view of the sad events of the last few days, they decided that leaving town was probably their best option. They thought that it was even probably divinely appointed. They told their landlord that they would not be renewing their lease. They told Onoja's office that they were willing to make the move.

The town they moved to was less cosmopolitan. Rent and other costs of living were cheaper. Keme found another job almost immediately. It was not as well-paying as her previous job, but the hours were much easier. The people here were also friendlier somehow. Even the weather seemed to be better than where they were coming from.

But all these changed in their second month of being there. Keme started feeling very sick, especially in the mornings. She found it difficult to drag herself out of bed and to work. Everything nauseated her, from the open sewer she had to pass if she decided to take a short-cut to work, to her husband's after-shave lotion which she had found quite enticing till then.

At first, the doctor at Onoja's workplace treated her for malaria. When she did not get better, he ran some tests that showed that she had "Borderline Typhoid", whatever that meant. He wrote out antibiotics for the typhoid and added some blood tonics, "Because you look rather pale" he explained.

In giving out the treatment, the lady pharmacists asked, "Are you pregnant?"

"I wish I were" Keme answered briefly.

"No, I'm serious" persisted the pharmacist. I need to know when you saw your period last before I fill this prescription for you."

"I frankly can't remember" Keme said, getting mildly irritated. "I will check it when I get home."

"In that case" said the pharmacist also getting irritated herself, "I strongly suggest that you go back to the doctor. Tell him about that before coming here to see me again."

Keme sighed at the tiresomeness of it all. Since she was still within the premises, she decided to go back to the doctor. The doctor was alarmed. He immediately ordered a pelvic scan for Keme. To her surprise, she found out that she was over two months pregnant! She worked it out in her mind and realized that ever since she lost her job and then her father, she had not seen her period. She just had not been thinking about it. She had been overwhelmed, trying to adjust to the changes around her including that of moving to a new town.

She whooped with joy! So, this was what was causing all her problems. These were the early pregnancy symptoms that her friends had described. She ran home. Her husband had to be told in a special way. He was excited too, but he said placidly, "I always knew that you worried too much about it. You needed to focus your worries on something else for it to happen."

"That was exactly what Mercy and Mike said" Keme concurred "I nearly ate them raw for it. I must call them and let them know."

She made lots of calls that night. Seven months late, she had her son. Two years later, his brother followed, and two years after that they had a sister. Keme says that her child-bearing days are over. Who knows? Now that she has taught herself to stop worrying about it, who knows what else may follow?

She is still very caring by nature. Onoja's influence has tempered her a lot. Nevertheless, people still think carefully before letting her know about anything. Some things never change in life.

RELAXATION

There are many stories about couples who having been married for several years without a child decide to adopt or to bring in another wife. And then the same month the baby, or the new wife arrives, the old wife just becomes pregnant, out of the blue.

The only explanation for this is the lifting of stress. Many women do not know that they are under stress from the constant expectation. One female author wrote, tongue-in-the-cheek, that the surest way of getting pregnant is to plan and expect not to be. The preface to this book talks of the many things that have to be normal for a pregnancy to occur, and to remain till delivery. Many of this "Normalcy" is orchestrated by what the doctors call "The higher centers". This is just the brain! The seat of whether a woman ovulates or not originates from an organ called The Hypothalamus which is located at the base of the brain. This is inadvertently influenced by the woman's thought patterns and perceptions! Under extreme stress, some women even stop menstruating. The stress of not having a baby could be so much that some women have mental problems.

Apart from psychological counseling (which hardly ever work even with the best experts), some people have suggested the use of anti-depressant and anti-stress medications. This author does not know of any scientific studies related to this but there is no doubt that some women undergoing psychological treatments get pregnant. On the other hand, some of the medications used in treating mental problems actually cause some of the hormones that prevent ovulation and therefore pregnancy to rise (See Index).

Artificial insemination, in-vitro fertilization and other techniques have been tried in such patients with varying success. Sustaining a pregnancy after conception has occurred must also have to do with the higher centers too. One thing that seems to work very well is getting the woman's attention focused on some other things. These might include community service, volunteer programs, fostering other people's children, adopting, and caring for another baby etcetera. These things have to do with focusing on other people's problems. As she does so, her own problems sort themselves out!

KEEPING IN SHAPE

*W*hat was it that made Bunmi to remain very slim? Nobody quite knew the answer to this. It could have been the fashions of the time, or that she did not want to become like her mother and her elder sisters. Everyone agreed, however, that Gbenga definitely had a lot to do with it.

Gbenga was always judging women by how fat he felt they were. He was always saying things like "She's so fat. I'm sure she sweats a lot!" Or "Such fatness must surely cause that woman to smell!" Or "She's truly heavy weight. Western suits will not fit her at all."

He even talked of men: "With such a fat belly, who knows whether he even waits on the Lord."

Even though such comments always seemed to pass Bunmi by, a lot must have settled into her sub-conscious mind. From the time they met, he had always complimented her on how slim she was. "Clothes sit well on you," he would say. "It's because you are slim and have a flat tummy."

He had been besotted with her wedding dress: "A fatter person would not have graced that dress. It brings out your shoulder so beautifully."

About one of her sisters he said, "She has become so fat. Only wrappers will ever fit her."

About another one of her sisters he said, "She should never wear skirt and blouse. It makes her tummy bulge in a disgusting way."

Even about his own sister he had said, "She is so mean. I'm sure she has a bad liver because she is this fat!" What Gbenga had to say about Bunmi's mother and about his own mother are not politely printable. His favorite aunt was probably that because "Even in her old age she still looked very trim and chic!"

There was just no way all this could not get to Bunmi. After all, she lived with him day after day, after day.

When Bunmi became pregnant, Gbenga was quite besotted with the thought of becoming a father. However, he kept hoping that "You will come back to shape after delivery. You must not become like one of those who stay permanently out of shape just because they had a baby,"

Bunmi did her best to watch what she ate. Her mother complained that she did not eat enough for a pregnant woman. Her mother-in-law plied her with all manner of mouth-watering dishes to tempt her to eat. Bunmi did her best to resist all the temptation. When she just could not bear it anymore, she would stuff herself with a lot of food and then lock herself in the toilet, stick two fingers down her throat and force herself to bring it all up again. Nobody knew of this practice, not even Gbenga. Whenever he was around, she tried not to stuff herself like that. Gbenga would stretch himself out in front of the television, cover his face with a newspaper and drawl in a lazy voice, "Don't let Mummy's cooking tempt you. You might put on so much weight that you cannot shed after you deliver."

The doctors were worried that Bunmi was not putting on any weight at all. She was a healthy, young woman in her first pregnancy. They did some tests and then told her that she was anemic. She lacked enough blood! "Are you sure that you are taking the blood builders that were prescribed for you?" they asked. Bunmi assured them that she was.

"Are you eating well?" they asked further. Bunmi said that she was trying her best.

"How can you be asking her that kind of question?" the nurse chaperone chided the doctor. "You reserve that kind of question for ignorant village women and poor peasants. Even those are now changing their attitudes to pregnancy, thanks to our daily health talks with them. This patient is a company secretary for crying out loud. Her husband is a banker! How can she not be eating well?"

"I have to ask," the poor doctor said in self-defense. "What else can account for this level of ancmia in this patient? This is her first pregnancy too?"

A barrage of tests was ordered for Bunmi. They all seemed normal except that her blood level was just too low. It was so bad that even the growth of the baby was terribly affected. Bunmi herself seemed to be going into heart failure. She had to be admitted. She was transfused with two unit of blood, just to tide her over.

While on admission, family and friends showered her with all manner of tempting dishes, vegetables, and fruits. The doctors and nurses saw all these by her bedside and assumed that she was feeding well. The truth of the matter was that Bunmi gave most of it away to the other patients. She tried to eat some of it but immediately afterwards she would go and shut herself into the toilet and induce vomiting. She would return to her bed looking very weak and wan. On questioning, she would admit to having been vomiting. The nurses dutifully reported this to the doctors who bent themselves over backward juggling her medications. They dropped some and added others all in efforts to stem the vomiting. Bunmi never admitted to anyone that she was artificially inducing the vomiting.

Gbenga on his part was genuinely concerned that his wife was sick enough to be on admission. He was worried that the baby was in danger, but he had great confidence in what modern medicine could do. He was not unduly alarmed. He came to see Bunmi at the hospital very frequently. He was overhead to make comments like, "So many people really love you. They show it in kind too. Just make sure you don't consume all of it and become fat."

Otherwise, he would say, "Go easy on the milk and eggs. You know they can be very fattening. You must not become Aunty Yoyo!"

Bunmi improved a lot after the transfusion. She was allowed home, but she went into labor two weeks later. The pregnancy was just entering its eighth month. The resultant baby boy was inevitably very small. He had to be kept in the special care unit for about a month. The labor went well for Bunmi. She did not lose a lot of blood. Thinking of the hazards of blood transfusion, the doctors said, "Her blood level is just borderline. She can build it up with good feeding and blood tablets."

But Bunmi was not feeding well at all. She continued her previous habit. It was a wonder how she was managing to survive. She was not producing enough breast milk for her son, Tobi. While at the hospital, artificial formula was prescribed for the boy just so he could survive. Under the doting eyes of his experienced grandmothers, he did so while they continued to complain about his mother.

Bunmi on the other hand was happy with the fact that even as she was leaving the hospital, she could wear her pre-maternity clothes with ease. Her mother-in-law said diplomatically, "You don't look as fresh as someone that has just delivered a baby."

Bunmi took it as a compliment especially when Gbenga said, "If not for these stretch marks, no one would have known that you have ever had a baby. That's my girl!"

By the time Bunmi resumed after her maternity leave, the care of Tobi fell more or less to her mother. Tobi played, fed, even bathed at Grandma's. His own mother came back from work each day very tired and worn out. She was only too glad that Tobi was already drowsy and ready for bed. If he was not, she would be so irritated and short with him. If he woke up in the night for anything, it was usually a chore to drag herself out of bed to attend to him. Most times it would be Gbenga that would wake up to get the odd cup of water, or tea, or to escort him to go to ease himself.

Mornings were always very hectic for them all. The adults rushed about to get to work on time. As time went on, it became even too much for Bunmi to bath and dress Tobi before taking him to her mother's. She began to take him there half asleep and still in his pajamas. She took spare clothing and dropped money to cover for feeding and other expenses. She and Gbenga usually ate at work. Not much cooking went on in their house anyway. There were all sorts of drinks in the refrigerator, and quick-fix foods in the cupboards. Gbenga often had to fix something for himself since Bunmi hardly ever ate. Tobi would have been fed at his grandma's.

To Gbenga, it was like a second return to bachelorhood. He was forever having to cook spaghetti or some other pasta for himself. Otherwise, he subsisted on bread and tinned fish. Every day, by the time he came back from work, his wife would be stretched out fast asleep on the bed. She did not seem to care that he too fell asleep in front of the television out of boredom.

The weekends were not much better. Increasingly Bunmi found it difficult to even get herself out of bed in the mornings. She had to go from lying down to swinging her feet out of bed, then sitting for some time before finally standing on her feet. If she did this too fast, she would become very dizzy and collapse. Her usual house chores lagged very much behind. It was quite unlike her. The house began to look neglected. Gbenga soon began to complain especially as it concerned caring for Tobi. Bunmi could hardly put herself together to perform the simplest tasks. Most times, she was either lying down on the bed or on the couch sleeping! Eventually the heaped clothing and the dirty house made them decide to employ a maid. The maid came in twice a week and matters improved a bit.

At the start of their marriage, Bunmi and Gbenga socialized a lot. They were always visiting or receiving visitors. This aspect of their life also suffered. Gbenga found himself having to go out alone more and more frequently. Bunmi usually pleaded "tiredness." Even when their friends visited, entertaining them was like a big chore to Bunmi. She soon became very sloppy at it, to the point of embarrassment.

Reading between the lines and not receiving reciprocal visits, their friends soon stopped coming around.

"You are neglecting this marriage," Gbenga complained bitterly once. "Nothing seems to interest you nowadays apart from your precious job. Even Tobi is suffering your neglect!"

Bunmi read him correctly. She did not have the energy to answer him back. "He thinks that I am having an affair at work," she told her sister later. The sister did not enlighten her that when a husband accuses one of having an affair, it was either because he was having one himself or seriously contemplating it. "The truth" continued Bunmi "is that I am not even enjoying my job. I seem to have lost a lot of interest in everything. I am always so perpetually tired."

Her work indeed was also suffering. Whereas she had always been so full of zest, one of the directors told her recently that "the spring seems to have gone out of your step."

One of her colleagues had asked her if she was pregnant again. "You seem to seize every opportunity to sit down. You look so gaunt and tired around your eyes!"

All these were true. She had worked very hard to shed weight after her pregnancy that she now weighed less than what she did even before she got married. This did not suit her at all. She looked rather unpleasant. Her head stood out prominently from the rest of her body. Her eyeballs and cheeks looked sunken. Her cheekbones and teeth stood out prominently in contrast. It made her look like someone going through the terminal stages of HIV-AIDS. Her sister told her so.

She had also wondered herself if she was pregnant again. She had taken adequate precautions because Gbenga was almost paranoid about it. "If this is what one baby can do to you, the next one will make a monster of you" he had said.

Her monthly periods had resumed two months after she delivered but the pattern had changed. The flow had reduced to three, then two, and now barely a day. At her sister's suggestion she had gone for urine testing. She had also done ultrasound scan, just to make sure she was not pregnant.

Her bosses began to complain more seriously about the quality of her work. It was human compassion, and her impeccable performance of the past that prevented her receiving queries. They felt something must be seriously wrong. They wondered how to intervene correctly because her inefficiency was also affecting the standard of the whole company.

Matters came to a head one day when it took her one full hour just to produce a letter. When she finally presented it, the managing director said harshly, "Finally! Bunmi you must decide whether you still want this job or not. We cannot continue to bear with you like this forever!"

Suddenly, Bunmi's eyes swam with tears. A red mist covered her vision. Even as she opened her mouth to try to apologize, she saw the ground coming up to meet her face. She passed out.

Everybody panicked. Bunmi was rushed to the hospital. A drip was set up immediately. A series of tests later, it was discovered that Bunmi still had severe shortage of blood. The specific cause of this could still not be determined. Some tentative treatments were commenced but Bunmi steadfastly refused another blood transfusion. She promised to eat better and build up her blood by herself.

Gbenga was strangely unsympathetic. He felt that Bunmi was "Faking the whole thing in order to get sympathy". He visited just once a day while she was on admission at the hospital. He usually came with Tobi and one other relative. His whole manner was somewhat aloof. "I think she just enjoys being sick, and all the attention that goes with it," he said to his sister, bitterly.

Bunmi was discharged after a week at the hospital. She did improve her eating habit. With all the vitamins and iron she was getting, she did begin to look healthier. The company sent a very official-looking letter stating that she could commence her annual vacation with pay. Afterwards, she could take as much time as she needed to get well, but without pay.

Bunmi had written such letters herself before. She knew what it really meant. She was politely being asked to resign from work if she felt that she could not cope. With how queerly her husband was behaving, she knew that she could not afford to lose her job as well. She therefore replied to the company with another official-looking letter of her own. She thanked them for their kind consideration but stated firmly that her doctors said that she would be fully recovered and able to resume work at the end of her vacation. She hassled the hospital for a medical report to this effect to go with her letter.

With this kind of motivation, she resumed in a very healthy state, almost back to her former self. She was even back to her former weight and wearing her former suits. She still ate sparingly, though better than before. She still had the habit of going to induce vomiting after an eating binge, occasionally.

Her marriage even improved somewhat. She kept the house better and managed to cook some meals. However, soon after her discharge from the hospital Gbenga came home one day and announced that he had been transferred to another town. "It's not so far away but I have to stay there the whole week so I can get to work on time. I will be home every weekend," he said.

It was good news for Bunmi in a way. Keeping Gbenga happy was becoming increasingly difficult. He seemed to believe that it was his tough attitude to Bunmi at the hospital that caused her to improve. Logically, tougher attitude should then bring greater improvement. The grandmothers were concerned on another score: "Tobi is almost three years old. Is it not time to plan a brother or a sister for him before the transfers become further and further away?"

Bunmi and Gbenga discussed this, and then started trying. A year later, they still had not succeeded. That was when they went to see the Gynecologist. Doctors have a way of asking intimate questions and getting answers. They dug up the facts of her first pregnancy, the blood transfusion, and the premature delivery. They even dwelt on the fact that she had not been able to breast-feed satisfactorily. They talked over their sex life which was limp and happened only on some weekends. They knowledgeably always tried to target her ovulation days, according to the books. Even her menstrual periods that had gradually reduced to, and remained at just a day also came under detailed scrutiny.

Gbenga and Bunmi were subjected to all manner of tests. At the end they were told that there was no medical reason why they should not have a baby. They received some medications and very useful advice but were essentially told to patiently keep on trying.

It was by accident that she watched a news-magazine program on satellite television as she was visiting her sister one day. Some American actresses who went to great lengths to remain slim were paraded. Theirs could have been her story but no one else knew. It was her secret life. The program concluded on the note of one of the actresses saying, "The doctors said that I might find it difficult, maybe even impossible to have a baby, but I don't care. I think my monthly periods are a nuisance anyway, and so would a baby be!"

That was where the actress definitely differed with Bunmi. Bunmi wanted another baby. She cared very much that something was wrong with her periods. She made discreet and indirect inquiries from her doctors and found out that her feeding habits could really be responsible for her problems. She tried very hard to change but the habit had become so deeply ingrained. She just could not help herself. She was still very finicky in her eating. She still went on binges occasionally, after which she would find herself locked inside one toilet with her fingers down her throat. She only seemed to come to her senses when she had been exhausted with the retching. She became desperate.

All this changed one day! Gbenga had been coming home less frequently. He pleaded "Pressure of work, sometimes extending to Saturdays and Sundays. Coming home in between, to go back to resume early Monday morning would be so strenuous."

Even when he was in town he was hardly home. There were friends to see and catch up with. There were meetings to attend. There were messages to deliver, and so on and so forth.

Bunmi was not naturally suspicious but very soon the rumors filtered back to her. Gbenga was keeping a married woman as a mistress at the other end of town. She did not confront him with it. She was not sure whether she believed it or not. On Friday however, she went with her colleagues to that side of town for the pre-nuptial celebrations of one of the office girls. Gbenga had phoned to say that he would not be home that weekend. He had some reports to finish and submit first thing on Monday morning.

To Bunmi's surprise, as they reached the Close where the ceremony was to hold, she saw Gbenga's car. She gasped audibly but pretended to her colleagues that it was something to do with her unmanageable headgear. At the peak of the ceremony, she slunk out to verify that it was really Gbenga's car. At that very moment, Gbenga himself emerged from the front door of the house. He got into the car and waited. The woman soon followed. She was carrying an overnight case. Bunmi gasped. She was stunned, not because she was catching Gbenga red-handed, nor because of the obvious implications of the overnight case. What surprised her was the appearance of Gbenga's *Objet d'amor*!

The woman was FAT! She was not just the polite over-weight of society. She was morbidly fat! Her legs and thighs were like tree trunks. Her belly was like a ceremonial cooking pot. Her neck had disappeared beneath rolls of fat which quivered as she walked. Her whole body strained from the very effort of moving. She was the exact opposite of Bunmi in every way. How could Gbenga love such a woman?

Bunmi became angry. She was angry at herself. She was angry at Gbenga. She was angry at the whole world. She never could tell how she left that place. The next thing she knew, she was in her mother's place, pouring out her heart about what she had seen. To her surprise, her mother seemed to know everything already, including who the other woman was. "The point is," said the older woman sagely, "now that you know, what do you intend to do about it? Do you want to give up on him or do you want to fight for him? Whatever it is that you decide to do, my advice is that you take time to think it all over first before you see Gbenga again."

Bunmi went on an eating binge. Automatically she went into the toilet afterwards but just as she was about to stick her fingers into her throat, she checked herself and said, "What the heck? The man pretends to like slim women and then goes out of his way to keep a fat mistress!" and then the tears came.

It would not be true to say that Bunmi was cured from then on. People spend a lot of money on treatment and psychological counseling and yet never get cured of this particular ailment. But Bunmi was a very strong woman. She was also very highly motivated. She persuaded her company to transfer her to where her husband was. They were only too willing to do so, with a promotion to boot. Gbenga was forced to find accommodation for his family. He was aided by the argument that he was having to "Work so hard there". The doctors had also been counseling it, if they really wished to have another baby.

It took close to another year, but Bunmi became a changed person in many aspects. She became more domestic despite, or perhaps because of, her promotion. She became more alluring. Gbenga found more reason to be home. They found time to always eat lunch together at home, with other things to follow. Gradually, Bunmi put on more weight. Her periods increased to two, then three, and then came back to four full days. About a year later, it was delayed for over a week. She went to the hospital, and it was confirmed. Bunmi was pregnant again. As the pregnancy advanced, it was discovered that Bunmi was carrying twins. Everyone was apprehensive but there was no need this time for hospital admissions. There was no need for blood transfusions. The twins came when they were expected: beautiful, fat, healthy and identical baby girls! Two years later, they also had a brother. Bunmi and Gbenga felt their family was now complete.

Today, Bunmi still gets the urge to stick her fingers down her throat. However, she squashes it. As one of her underlings put it, "Madam is so pleasantly plump and looks good whether in suits or in native attire."

She never did confront Gbenga with his affair with Fatso. He has also never been known to have any other affairs to date. He seems so happy and content with his plump wife. "No," he had been heard to say, "She is not what she used to be when I married her. She is so much better! Am I not taking good care of her?"

IN SHAPE

The global trend in the world these days is to worship the slim body. Unfortunately, changing dietary patterns, sedentary occupations, and even sedentary modes of recreation has also increased the global trend of obesity. Those that are overly concerned about their body weight find themselves suffering from eating disorders like Anorexia Nervosa (Picking at one's food and not getting enough sustenance), or Bulimia (Gorging oneself on inappropriate food and then going to induce vomiting so that the food does not digest). In between these two are other such eating disorders which might not be so serious. Even children tend to suffer from them these days.

The World Health Organization says that a person's ideal weight is determined by his or her Body Mass Index (BMI). The BMI is got by dividing the weight (in Kilograms) by the height (in meters) and again dividing the result by the height in meters again [Weight in KG/ height in meters squared]. A BMI of eighteen to twenty-five is alright. Lower than eighteen is underweight, and higher than twenty-five is overweight. Higher than thirty is obese and lower than twelve is seriously underweight. This means that logically, different people are supposed to weigh different things and still be healthy – logically!

A person's weight is made up of the weight of the bones, the muscles, the fat and water! Men have more bone and muscle mass than women. It is the fatty mass in women that give them their more curvaceous shapes. Nature has so made it that there is a weight that a young girl must reach before she starts menstruating. Not only should she reach about forty-five kilograms, at least forty percent of this weight must be fat! Anything less than this, a woman tends to have problems with her menstruation and reproduction – ask professional athletes whose body masses are more muscle than fat. To get pregnant, some of them are best advised to retire and reduce their strenuous training.

Even at the other extreme of life, nature again causes that women tend to put on weight just before menopause. This helps to continue estrogen production even after menopause. This is necessary for a healthier life even in old age (See **The Changing Tides** *by this same author).*

Eating disorders are notoriously very difficult to treat. It requires a willingness to adjust, and the discipline to break an ingrained habit. The shock that Bunmi had in catching her husband with another woman was a very necessary trigger for her rehabilitation. Unfortunately, emotional shocks are never pleasant, but they can be very useful like in this case.

MISS YOUNG

*G*race did not get married early even though she was bright, attractive, intelligent, out-going, industrious ...in short, she was everything that young men claimed to be looking for in a wife. One thing was for sure, it was not for lack of suitors. Even when she was still a baby, many a mother was known to claim her for their sons. They would usually tell her mother, "Look after our wife well. We shall be coming in a few years to claim her."

Or they would give her gifts or do services for her parents free of charge. They would then say, "Oh! We are just reducing the dowry that we will have to pay when the time comes to marry her for our son."

Of course, most of these were in jest. In jest also like most children were wont to do, she got married at different occasions to her playmates. Of course, such marriages usually ended with the particular play sessions they happened in. They were usually not counted as anything afterwards.

When she was nine years old or so, she developed a giant crush on a twenty-five-year-old civil servant that always came to stay with their neighbor during his vacations. Everyone started calling her "Mike's wife". To this she responded with such extreme shyness, sometimes bursting into tears. Her mother had to put a stop to such teasing. After some time, it all passed, and life went on.

Her mother was a real asset. She was one of those paragons that happened on earth about once every generation to any particular locality. Grace was especially close to her, being the first child, and the only girl of the four children. They were often referred to as sisters. In fact, she died while trying to have a sister for Grace. It was very painful, but they named the baby girl Comfort. Grace considered Comfort a very special gift from her mother.

"Anyway," remarked one of the neighbors that came to commiserate, "such goodness never lasts for long. She was too good for this world."

Everybody was devastated, twelve-year old Grace not the least of all. They rallied with time. About a year after her death, her widower tried to remarry. "The loneliness is excruciating," he explained, "and I do need help with the children."

Grace begged him not to remarry. She recounted to him all the stories they had ever shared about wicked stepmothers. Nobody else was willing to come and help with the children. Their aunts were busy with their own families. Their grandfathers were very reluctant to let their grandmothers go. Even the cousins that had enjoyed coming to stay with them when their mother was alive were loath to come now that she was dead.

At last, a willing and needy distant cousin was found. They had respite for some time but having prevented her father from remarrying, young Grace felt that the onus was on her to look after her siblings. She did so very admirably. She did a good job too. She ran the house. She kept herself and her siblings clothed and fed. She supervised their schoolwork as well as kept up with her own.

The "supervising" cousin did little more than take politely given orders from Grace even though she was actually a few years older. After some time, she grew heady. She was driven by her hormones to chase boys all over the neighborhood. Friends called Grace's father and advised him to better send the lady home. "Otherwise, she will get pregnant in your house one day and accuse you of being responsible."

Another person counseled, "Think of how she is influencing your daughters. They will soon begin to think that this is the right way to behave."

The advice was timely. Grace's father sent the girl home. Just a few months after she left, she had a misadventure and was found to be pregnant. She fingered one man who was forced to marry her even though he tried to deny the responsibility. It was a narrow escape for Grace's family. No other person was brought to come to live with them.

Shortly afterwards, Grace's father also died. Some people said he died of a broken heart and loneliness. He left the five children as orphans. Grace was just nineteen years. She had been hoping to go to university to study Accounting. She convinced herself that it would be better for herself and for her siblings if she went to Nursing School instead. The years of study were shorter. Nurses were also paid stipends as students in training. The gratuity from her father's company and the donations by generous individuals during his burial was much. Wisely, she knew that these would not last for long. She decided to put it all aside in a fixed deposit account for her brothers' schooling. The said brothers were then aged sixteen, fourteen, and twelve years. Comfort was seven years. Grace counted her as her own special responsibility.

Grace rose admirably to the challenge. She did her best to provide for their daily need and other minor needs. Apart from the stipends paid by the school, she engaged in petty trading from their doorstep. She dealt in anything from ice water and ice blocks to fruits and beaded jewelry. She hired herself out in her spare time to cook, to clean, or to baby-sit.

When she finished her studies at the school of nursing, she got a job immediately. She still did not give up looking for other ways of making money. She only changed from the menial and the mundane to the chic and stylish. Someone said that she changed from picking pennies to making pounds. That was a picturesque way of describing it but those were the bare facts.

"I don't even know why she puts herself through all that stress" said one well-meaning relative of hers to others. "All she has to do is get married. Her husband and in-laws would have then helped her to carry the burden."

The listeners nodded their heads sagely. Only rarely would one venture to suggest that Utopia was not always so. People were more often than not on the look-out for who would help carry their burdens, not whose burdens they would help to carry.

"Oh yes!" the original speaker might rejoin, "But there are many good people from many good families willing to marry her; wanting to marry her; even begging to marry her!"

And indeed, there were. But as well-meaning as these her relatives were, if the truth were to be told they had not lifted their hands nor donated any reasonable resources to help her and her siblings. These people that were willing, and wanting, and begging, to marry her often wanted her for some weak-kneed son of theirs. They knew how industrious and responsible Grace had proven to be. Grace was quite clear-sighted about it. "I am not yet ready to marry," she always said unequivocally. "I will let everybody know once I am."

On her off-duty days as a nurse, Grace discovered that she could travel far to buy merchandise that she could sell at home at a considerable profit. She volunteered to be on permanent night – a duty that other nurses shied away from. The hospital management was grateful for that. She started a long rotation of three days on, and four days off. Night duties were not always very busy. During the day when she could, she would run around for her businesses. On her off-duty days, she would travel to buy goods.

Grace became quite wealthy, but she was still very modest. She invested much of what they did not strictly need. She lived at home with Comfort while the boys went to boarding schools, and thereafter to the University. During one of her annual vacations, she discovered that she too could enroll as a part-time student at a university. She thought that she had always wanted to be an accountant. When she saw the advertised courses however, she decided on the spur of the moment to enroll for Law. She calculated that this would take her a total of six years. It was also quite expensive, but she could afford it. It would allow her time to pursue her other businesses while still working as a nurse. She enrolled immediately.

The year that she graduated, two of her brothers also graduated and went for Youth Service. Grace at thirty-two was too old to serve. By then her relatives doubted if she would ever get married. "She has become too independent," said one, "She will never be able to live under a man."

"Yes," said another, "Who would want to go for ladies that are over-thirty, when "sweet sixteens" are available?"

But someone wanted to marry Grace. Felix was her classmate at the Law School. He was also a self-made businessman. He was putting himself through school "in order to add some polish", as he explained. He proposed to Grace. Although Grace liked him a lot as a person and for his industriousness, she hesitated. "I have some work at hand right now. I shall consider marriage only after it's all over" she parried.

"Are you stupid?" asked her best friend, Blessing. "This is the kind of person you have been waiting for all your life. You should jump into it at once or someone else will snap him up."

"In that case," replied Grace with infuriating coolness, "it was not meant to be. If it is meant to be he will wait for me till I am ready."

At thirty-five years of age, Grace was finally ready to marry. Two of her brothers were already married and standing on their own. The youngest brother had just finished Youth Service and was on the verge of landing a very lucrative job. Her baby sister, her mother's special gift to her, the birth of whom had also ended their mother's life, was almost out of school. A charming young doctor had come to thank Grace one day for all that she had done in Comfort's life. He had then proceeded to ask for Grace's permission to woo Comfort.

Grace liked the young man. She felt that he would be just right for Comfort, so she had given them her blessing. The day that Comfort graduated, the young doctor was there in full force to support her. Grace attended the ceremony with Felix. In the emotions of the peak of the moment, Felix proposed again. This time, with a sense of mission accomplished, Grace agreed. Without a father nor a mother she had made something of herself and of all her siblings. She definitely would like someone else to take care of her.

There was nothing to wait for. They did not even plan a flamboyant wedding. They had a simple registry wedding. Only their immediate family was present. Almost immediately, she became pregnant and gave birth to her son Willie. She named the boy after her father. Willie was breast-fed for a full year! While she was breast-feeding him, Grace did not see her period. Everybody assured her that this was normal. After she stopped breast-feeding, her period did not still resume. At first, she hoped that she was pregnant. When urine tests and ultrasound scans kept showing that she was not pregnant, she went to the hospital to find out what was wrong. She went from doctor to doctor. She did innumerable tests. Sometimes she was given some types of medications that would cause her to see her period for that month only. She knew this was not enough for her to become pregnant.

At last, when Willie was about two years old, she met a doctor that did some blood tests. He assured her that this was indeed menopause. Menopause? She was not even forty yet!

Felix said that he did not mind having just the one son as long as they had each other. They thanked God daily for Willie who turned out to be like more than ten sons in one. At first, he minded not having brothers and sisters. "Other children have brothers and sisters. Where are mine?" He used to harass his mother with "When will you get brothers and sisters for me?" His parents used to answer with what he always considered unsatisfactory platitudes.

When he grew a bit older his song changed to, "When I grow up, I will marry and have lots of children. They will become my brothers and sisters!"

At nineteen, and just in his second year in the university he brought a girl home. He introduced the girl to his mother as the person he intended to marry. He held his breath and waited for the usual parental explosion about how stupid and how irresponsible a move he was trying to make. It did not come. What he got instead was a surprise recount of the story of his mother's life. Grace concluded by saying, "So if I had not married your father when I did, who knows, I may have lost all my chances of ever having a baby of my own. People would have insisted that it was a just punishment for my refusing to marry early."

Willie graduated at twenty-three with a first class in Accountancy. He proceeded to immediately marry the girl he had introduced to his mother. He did not delay in starting a family. He kept her busy producing babies in such quick succession that his parents had to step in and plead for his wife's life. They stopped at six, but he threatened, "It's not as if we don't want more, we are just taking a break for now."

AGEING

Bunmi (Keeping in Shape) was under a lot of physical stress, while Keme (Stress and Distress) was under a lot of mental stress. Here we see Grace under what is best described as social stress.

*Researchers are still looking into the factors that influence the age at which a woman ceases to menstruate. Menopause after the age of thirty-five is no longer considered as premature. Generally, though, it **naturally** occurs between the ages of forty-five and fifty-two.*

*It is easier to classify, and even quantity the factors that influence the age at which girls begin to see their periods. However, at this stage the most that has been stated are the factors that seem not to influence when the periods cease. In Nigeria for one, data has been extremely difficult to obtain because of poor record-keeping. Many women could not even say for sure when they were born. What can be said for sure so far is that the age of onset of menses does not affect when they cease. The number of pregnancies in the woman's lifetime does not affect when menses stop. The contraceptive method(s) the woman used does not affect it either. The exception perhaps is the tying of the tubes but even that is still being debated. Where a woman lived or worked, her race or her creed, the weather, and other physical factors seem to have no influence on when she stops seeing her period compared with her peers. (See **The Changing Tides** by this same author).*

One definitely related factor is the presence of body-wasting diseases like Diabetes, Tuberculosis, HIV-AIDS, different cancers, and such things. These tend to bring about an early menopause, but this is usually when the disease raged on uncontrolled, or as a result of the treatment method adopted. Cigarette-smoking is also associated with early menopause.

In a group of women that had been followed up for a long time, some researchers noticed that girls that lost either of their parents early, either to death or due to divorce attained menopause earlier than the others. The explanation for this cannot yet be found.

These days however, menopause need not be the end of childbearing (See Index). Some assisted reproductive techniques still force retired ovaries to produce eggs, and some other women get donor eggs. The lesson however still remains that people should strive to have their children as early in life as possible because one never knows what tomorrow may hold.

PATIENT SELECTION

"*H*ad I known..." is a phrase that everyone acknowledges always comes last. Perhaps if it learnt to come first, many disasters would have been averted in this world.

That was what Zigwai and Malgwi also said. They were also practical enough to know that such regrets never changed anything, so they moved on with their lives, nevertheless.

That fateful morning, there had been a message from the village. Zigwai's mother was very sick. This was not the first time that she had become sick like this. The only difference this time was that she was asking for Zigwai and Malgwi to come and see her together, "Urgently!"

That was so unlike her. She was an unassuming woman who never interfered in their marriage except to give a little advice here, and a little encouragement there. The last time she had visited however, Zigwai and Malgwi had an uncharacteristic and very loud argument. It was not just before her, but before their daughters too. The whole thing seemed to have been centered on the fact that Zigwai was having only baby girls. They had different cultural backgrounds. Malgwi also wanted son! Zigwai kept accusing her husband of having an affair in order to get the needed boy. Malgwi denied this steadfastly, but something was very fundamentally wrong. This had never been an issue with them at all. They were such a well-suited couple. They never argued publicly till that day.

That was two months before. Mama had gone back to the village very distraught. She was hypertensive but had been doing well on her medications. Three mornings before, however, she had a small stroke. The force of her mortality was brought back to her. She counted the loose ends she might be leaving behind if she died then. Zigwai and Malgwi were part of them. She wanted to leave them with some last words, hence the message.

The quarrel had festered for the past two months. Malgwi had always been the perfect gentleman, "to a fault," Zigwai always said. "That is why people always take advantage of him."

When the message from Mama came, there was no question, but that Zigwai would manouvre herself into the car with her protuberant tummy. Malgwi drove her the one hour or so to the village to see Mama at once!

Yes, Zigwai was heavily pregnant with their fourth baby. They all hoped would be a baby boy. It was the snide remark of a neighbor about those that "Incessantly bore girls" that had sparked off the quarrel of two months before. They said regrettable things to each other in front of their girls and Mama. Now the quarrel all forgotten, they were united in their anxiety for Mama.

Malgwi drove faster than usual in his anxiety, but he was a very careful driver. That was why he saw the stationary bus on time. Fresh leaves had been strewn on the ground to show there was danger up ahead. Just as they turned the corner, there was the bus! It was an eighteen-seater bus. Since the road was not that busy, the passengers had alighted. They were sitting by the roadside while the driver and his mate worked on the bus.

Malgwi slowed down as they got closer. "Was it an accident?" he asked absent-mindedly. "Should we stop to help?"

"It doesn't look like an accident" Zigwai answered tonelessly. "They seem to be stranded though, and rather far from any help."

Even as they speculated on whether they could be of help or not, a big luxurious bus swept round the corner. The driver had either not noticed, or did not really think that the strewn leaves meant anything. A little too late, he saw the damaged vehicle. He saw the other vehicles trying to get past it in a skewered line. He also saw the passengers sitting around it. He tried to brake, swerved off the road; came back to it again, and swerved again. The bus then came down on its side, on top of three other vehicles including the damaged bus, Zigwai's car, and a pick-up truck in between the two. It fell on top of the passengers that were sitting by the roadside, the driver and his mate that were trying to repair the bus, and its own forty or so passengers went tumbling on top of one another like a ton of bricks.

Less than a minute! That was what it took to change the lives of these people forever. There were over seventy people involved. The noise of the accident had been deafening. Even though the road was not a busy one, nor was there a village close by, within minutes the scene was full of people trying to help. Other road users and the uniformed men arrived. The nearest health facility was a government hospital about ten kilometers away. People offered their vehicles, and the victims were moved immediately. Thankfully there were no fires. Everyone was rescued including those that were trapped.

The small hospital was overwhelmed. It had admission facilities for over a hundred people, but it was terribly under-staffed. It was also handicapped by lack of equipment. At that moment though, there was a doctor on duty; two nurses; two ward aids, and a security man. They had just been complaining of idleness when the mass casualties started arriving. They rose to the occasion with a great deal of zeal. Little did they know that they would still be on their feet and working twenty-four hours later.

"First," said the doctor, "we must separate the dead from the living."

It sounded so callous and too matter of fact but everyone knew this was the truth. The dead were beyond help. They would encumber those that could still be saved. Fifteen people were very obviously dead. The security guard was told to direct volunteers to take these to the mortuary. There were about eighteen people that seemed to have no injuries at all. These were co-opted to help until the doctor could check them more thoroughly.

"Sister" said the doctor, addressing the senior of the two nurses, "see to the ones that have minor cuts and fractures. You can work on those with the ward aids."

Sister was very efficient and undaunted. Briskly she held out pads to those that were bleeding and told them to hold these over the cuts and apply some pressure. She instructed a ward aid to prepare a table and they started suturing the bad lacerations. "Got out the splints" she told the other ward aid. "We shall temporarily set the compound fractures. There were about two of these. They then turned to suturing the lacerations and arresting hemorrhages. Of these, there were many.

The doctor found a laboratory technician among the casualties. He had a sprained ankle which the doctor bandaged. He then recruited the young man to help him with the more serious casualties. Most of these were unconscious. Zigwai was one of them. She was breathing erratically. Her husband sat beside her on the ground asking every passer-by "Please help us. Can you do anything for my wife?"

He himself had sustained a sprained wrist and a cut above his left eye. The cut had stopped bleeding by itself. None of these bothered him. What bothered him was that his wife seemed to be dying right before him and he could do nothing about it. The doctor and his assistant reached them. "This one ought not to be lying on her back" he said. Directing his assistant, they deftly turned her to lie on her side. He gasped, "Oh my God! This one is pregnant too!"

"She is eight months gone" Malgwi supplied, grateful for her improved breathing. "What else can I do to help her?"

"Nothing else for now" replied the doctor. "We shall return to her later." They continued down the line, seeing to the other injured patients. Malgwi nodded. He continued to sit beside his wife. He did not know who to call, nor how. Nobody knew their whereabouts. It was twelve full hours before they came back to Zigwai again. Within that period four more people had died. A lot more had been saved. With the help of the uniformed men, others that were considered very critical had been moved to the bigger hospital in town.

"Your wife seems to be doing well" said the doctor to Malgwi as he squatted beside Zigwai to check her. "Perhaps we should move her to the wards."

"I don't know" Malgwi replied cautiously. "She seems to be in pain. Every now and then her breathing would increase, and she would groan aloud."

As if to buttress his point, Zigwai began to groan then. The rate of her breathing did increase.

"Hmm," observed the doctor. "This is interesting."

"Could she be in labour?" Malgwi ventured.

"It's a possibility. In fact, it's probable. "I have not really examined her in the light of her pregnancy. We were more concerned with saving her life first." To the ward aids he said, "Come give me a hand. Let us turn her on her back again. Lift her unto the couch."

Before Malgwi could ask his next question, they were already doing this. That was when they saw that she had been lying in a pool of blood! They were galvanized into immediate action. Within the minute, she was in the minor surgical theatre. "A drip!" commanded the doctor. "Set up normal saline for her now!"

"We're out of drips," said the junior nurse.

"I saw you take one out a few minutes ago" Sister insisted. Go and get it."

"That was a dextrose infusion" she replied. "Doctor is asking for normal saline."

"Get whatever is available" the doctor said. "We need to get some fluid into her NOW!"

The junior nurse left. She took her time coming back. Even then, it was only to say that she could not find the drip anywhere. By this time Zigwai was moaning continuously. When they finally managed to undress her sufficiently, it was just on time. Quickly, they put her in position. With a shuddering heave, she pushed her fresh stillborn son to the outside world. The placenta came out with the baby, as well as a large clot of blood. Zigwai herself was still unconscious. And then the real bleeding started.

It was as if a tap was opened. She started pouring blood. The doctor rubbed and rubbed. At a stage it seemed to Malgwi that he put his whole hand inside his wife's womb to try to control the bleeding. He kept barking out orders to the nurses and the aids. He made them run and come back with one thing after another. Through it all he kept moaning: "A drip! If only we had a drip! If we cannot give her blood, we should be giving her something else at least."

All they had was taken up by the day's mass casualty already. Malgwi looked on helplessly. He wept like a baby. Nobody had remembered to ask him to go out. He saw every other person scuttling about and wondered what he could do to at least help. He saw that Zigwai could possibly die. He wondered how his life would be without her. He stumbled into the night and collapsed on the grass beneath the window while the valiant staff struggled to save his wife. "God," he wept, "oh God spare my wife! Please spare her for me! I cannot do without her, God. Please don't let her die yet."

He pleaded with God. He made all manner of promises and bargains with The Almighty. God was surely paying attention. Suddenly one of the ward aids rushed past him, apparently pursued by the junior nurse. Something seemed to be happening and Malgwi got up to look. The ward aid thrust something to the doctor and said what sounded like, "She was hiding it. I picked it from where she hid it!"

The junior nurse opened her mouth and closed it several times. The doctor just gave her a withering look. She turned and went away with her head bowed. The doctor muttered something like, "I hope this will help." He proceeded to set up what Malgwi saw was a drip. He added some injections to it. Malgwi saw that there was also a tube in Zigwai's nose through which the other ward aid also seemed to be giving her something. He also saw that Zigwai was breathing. The bleeding seemed to have stopped.

It was a long night. Before daybreak, the doctor sent for an ambulance that took Zigwai to the big hospital in the city. There, blood transfusion was started immediately. This hospital commended the doctor and his team for a job well done. They commiserated with Malgwi over the loss of his son. Frankly he said, "It doesn't matter. I'm so glad my wife is alive. That is the most important thing." He meant every word of it. He continued to mean it till the end of his life.

Zigwai did recover, as did many other people from that accident. She consoled her husband, "at least we have proven that we can make a baby boy together. Another one will come."

But Zigwai did not get pregnant ever again. She did not even resume her menses again. Her breast did not produce milk as it should have after that baby. She did a lot of tests and was told that it was because of the bleeding during the accident. She ate well and took lots of blood-builders. Even though she made a lot of blood, "enough to even donate to others twice a month" one laboratory technologist told her, she still did not menstruate. At last, she did one test that showed that truly, at twenty-eight, Zigwai had attained menopause. There was nothing anybody could do about it.

Mama lived on for two more years after this event, and Malgwi for over thirty years. All their daughters got married. Between the three of them, they gave their parents ten grandsons, and only one granddaughter. People said it was the effect of all the prayers that their mother had said all those years for baby boys. Zigwai herself is still alive. Her face had begun to wrinkle like an old woman's when she was still in her early thirties. A doctor told her that it was because she was no longer menstruating. He also said it was not a matter of cosmesis alone. Her bones and heart were also in real danger. He prescribed some medications that caused Zigwai to "artificially" see her menses every month. She had also been warned to take breaks in between, and never to take them without supervision. She took them till her mid-fifties, and then stopped permanently. She is the first to always admit that life has not dealt her too bad a hand.

CHOOSING

This story was included to show how such minute decisions can affect someone's fertility for life. Who was to be held responsible for Zigwai's problems? Even the junior nurse could not have known the extent of the damage her hiding the drip could have had. Was it that one single drip that really saved her? Probably not! Besides, the blood loss was long-standing. The damage was probably already done before Zigwai was noticed as an extreme emergency.

With all bias, in a mass emergency like this, women should be given a higher priority than men. Pregnant women should be given higher priorities still! This is because they are at a rather delicate stage. Further than that, more than one life is involved.

Childbirth is just one of the ways in which women could lose blood in dangerous quantities. This could be to an extent that affects one of the very sensitive organs of the brain concerned with fertility and other things, if not corrected at once. Bleeding fibroids (See **The Tales of Ten Women** *by this same author), ruptured spleen or liver, or even accidental cut to the arms or legs that bleed a lot could also cause this problem.*

When this sensitive organ shuts down, it just refuses to be resuscitated again. Its functions just have to be supplemented by medications given for the duration of the woman's lifetime. So far, what could be done to get the woman pregnant again has not been found but medical science is still working on it. There is a new line of medications that is showing some promise. In any event, they may benefit from assisted reproduction as menopausal women. Even then, the responses are not that good.

The essence of replacing those hormones in Zigwai was not just to get her pregnant. They were also to protect the heart and bone changes that begin to manifest after menopause. In the event, not only did she outlive her mother, she also outlived her husband. She lived to see her many grandsons!

Pregnancy might not be everything in life. However, it sure feels good to know that one helps a woman preserve her fertility.

OF WITCHES AND WIZARDS

*W*hen Sim learnt that she was pregnant for the second time she did not believe it. First of all, she did not feel pregnant at all. Her first pregnancy had been turbulent. The early pregnancy symptoms had been terrible. She vomited till she collapsed. She could not keep down anything, not even water. At a stage she had to be admitted for two weeks at the hospital. She had to be sustained by intravenous infusions. Now ultrasound scan indicated that she was already four months pregnant. Four months of absolutely no inconvenience!

The second reason that she would not believe that she was pregnant was that her baby was just eleven months old. She had not even resumed her menses since after having him. Jenom was still breast-feeding. Sim's mother and aunts had told her that breastfeeding "seriously" was a way of warding off pregnancy. She had taken their advice. According to the ultrasound report, she had become pregnant when her baby was just seven months old despite the fact that she was breast-feeding very "seriously"! What would people say?

This was the third reason for her not believing that she was pregnant: what people would say. She had joined to tease her other colleagues and friends that became pregnant soon after a delivery. "You must like your husband too much. Couldn't you have said 'No' to sex so soon after delivery?" or things along such lines. Now it was her turn to be teased.

Sim was in self-denial. It was a natural reaction to shock. However, whether she believed it or not, the baby was there, and was stubbornly growing. The doctor counseled her to continue breastfeeding if she wanted to. "There is no danger to the baby inside the womb, nor to the one outside. You just have to feed well. Eat lots of calcium-containing foods because both of them will be demanding a lot from you."

"What if I choose to stop breast-feeding?" She asked. "I had hoped to breast-feed for about two years according to the Baby Friendly Program."

"If you choose to stop breast-feeding, don't feel guilty about it at all. Your baby is already eating other things," the doctor told her. "Just make sure there is enough protein in his meals so that he doesn't get kwashiorkor."

After listening to the doctor, Sim also had to hear her mother out. "You must stop breast-feeding at once!" Mama said emphatically. "Who knows what harm has been done to Jenom already? Everybody knows that the breast milk of a pregnant woman is poisonous. It can kill her baby. Maybe that is why Jenom is not yet walking. My own babies walked at nine months, or at most ten months."

Her aunts added their own voices. They had many stories to tell about people that this kind of thing had happened to. "Continue to breast feed while you are pregnant? This is madness indeed."

Sim wavered between the two opinions. She found it difficult to make up her mind on whose advice to follow: the doctor whose knowledge came from reading textbooks, or her kinswomen whose knowledge was based on years and years of experience. Her mind was made up for her when Jenom developed severe diarrhea and vomiting. He had to be admitted to the hospital and put on intravenous infusions and special feeding. At a stage a tube was passed through his nose into his stomach for medications and for feeding. He was too weak to even suckle. He spent ten days altogether at the hospital and at the end of this period he was inadvertently weaned. By the time he was discharged, Sim now had to tend the baby inside the womb and the one outside separately. A few days after discharge, Jenom was also wobbling about on unsteady feet. Mama had nothing to complain about again.

Sim's tummy grew. Five months after all the hullabaloos began, she gave birth to a beautiful baby girl. They named her Senom. O people had talked and castigated Sim and Nom for having no self-control. During the dedication, however, when the pastor offered to throw Senom away since she was not a planned baby, there was a universal and throaty "Noooo…"

Senom might not have been planned, but she was definitely wanted. She was very welcome indeed. "Better find out what other women do so that the whole world doesn't get to know whenever their husbands play with them" Nom said to his wife.

And so, by-passing her mother and her aunts this time, Sim went to the Reproductive Health Clinic. After an extensive counseling, she decided to start using the three-monthly injections. It was very convenient – just four times every year. Jenom and Senom grew. Sim had time to think of going back to school without fear of pregnancy. Nom was also happy with the arrangement. He complained that his wife was putting on weight from the injections. "You are beginning to look quite chubby," he told her on several occasions.

"People will think that you are taking good care of me" was Sim's reply.

Senom's fourth birthday corresponded with Sim's final examinations. They agreed this was a good time to stop the family planning injections and "Try for our last-born". She did not go to renew the injection when it was due. Three months passed. Sim lost a lot of weight. She was again looking like her previous trim and beautiful self before she started on the injections. Six months passed but Sim's monthly periods did not resume. She had been warned before she started on the injections that she might have menstrual irregularities. For some women their menses might even cease altogether. When Sim did not see her period for the four years that she was on the injection, she counted it a great advantage. Now however, she was eager for it to resume. She wanted her last born nine months after her last injection. She finally became worried enough to go to the hospital and complain. A few tests were done. She was given medications and reassured. The very next month, Sim's menses resumed, and she was happy.

Her menses were very regular, in fact too regular. She wanted to miss it so that she would know that she was pregnant, but this did not happen. Regular menses and a pregnancy did not normally go together. She went back to the hospital. This time, her major complaint was that her menses was coming too regularly. She wanted a baby!

The doctor asked all the usual embarrassing questions, did some tests including a womb x-ray. At last, she was told that there was nothing basically wrong with her. There was no reason why she could not have a baby. She was placed on some medications that had some unpleasant side-effects and told that these would probably induce or enhance ovulation in her. Sim wanted a baby, so she took the medications very diligently and very stoically. Still, she did not get pregnant.

A year passed. Sim decided to take a break from taking medications. She turned to prayers instead. She never missed going for any prayers for women desiring to get pregnant and yet the miracle did not happen for her. Her mother tried to get her to take native medications. "They are not fetish," she tried to persuade her daughter. "They are merely herbs and minerals that were known to the ancients from long ago. You never know how God may choose to work."

Sim was sorely tempted to try but she did not yield to the temptation. Her mother went to consult the medicine man on her behalf anyway. She found out that the root cause of all her problems was a jealous in-law. Sim would not listen to her expatiate. She refused to encourage her to look for more explicit answers or solutions. Sim however did allow herself to be persuaded to try some Chinese and Indian herbal preparations imported from America. It was the current rave among her colleagues and contemporaries. Still, she did not get pregnant.

After another year passed, she decided to try another Gynecologist. This doctor asked more searching questions. Sim's use of the three-monthly injections emerged, as well as the fact that she had been having blinding headaches recently. "I think they are tension headaches," she said. "I learnt some relaxation exercises recently and I think they are helping."

When the doctor asked if she was still discharging milk from her nipples, Sim laughed and said "I stopped breast-feeding eight years ago. My baby is almost ten years old!"

When the doctor was examining her however, quite a spurt of milk came from her nipples. Sim was very surprised. Demonstrating to Nom at home later, he said "I had noticed it before, but I thought it was normal."

"Of course, it is not that normal" said Sim's mother much later when she heard about it. "Before your breasts start squirting milk like that, you have just had a baby, or you had it specially washed and a baby sucking on it. I told you but you would not listen. It's our enemies that are doing this. They have probably given you a baby in the spirit world and made it impossible for you to have any in the physical world. This is witchcraft but you will not listen to your old mother. You and your modern ways!" and she spat on the ground in disgust.

Sim wondered why she had even bothered to mention it to her mother. However, this was her mother after all. That night, she dreamt that she was breast-feeding a bizarre shapeless baby. She woke up shivering. However, she determined that she would rather follow her "Foolish modern ways" than her mother's superstitious ways. She asked the doctor what she needed to do. The doctor ordered additional tests including some expensive blood tests and x-rays of the skull. Compared to the tests Sim had done before, these ones were not uncomfortable in the least. She was started on another course of medications. As she told her friend, "They were very tiny medicines, compared to the ones I had taken before, but they are so mighty. If I take them without eating, the world will turn round and come crumbling around me."

Sim was willing to go to any extent the doctors told her. She kept reminding herself that the alternative was to recourse to what her mother planned. Gradually she got used to the medications. She no longer felt anything when she took them. She had been warned by the doctor and some friends that the more she pressed her nipples, the more the milk would be flowing. She had stopped pressing to check. She left it only to whenever she went for her check-ups.

The breast milk changed from white to colorless. It was still coming much though. It then became gradually less until the day the doctor pressed and got nothing at all. The doctor felt that this was a major improvement. He encouraged Sim to continue on the medication for a while longer.

He had an irritating habit of beginning each consultation by asking Sim to recall when she saw her menses last, and how it had gone. Due to pressure at work and some traveling around, Sim had misplaced her diary. She searched for it frantically the day before her appointment because that was where she had noted how her period went. At last on a calendar, she had also made a note of it the previous month, she saw that her period ought to have come the week before, no, ten days before! It had never happened like that before. Could it be? Could it actually be? She went for her doctor's appointment trying to contain her excitement. As soon as she mentioned the delayed period, the doctor was, if anything even more excited than she was. The tests were called for immediately. It was confirmed. Sim was really pregnant!

"Will the medications affect the baby?" she asked.

"Definitely not," answered the doctor. "In fact I think you should continue it for a few more months.

When Senom was twelve years old, and Jenom almost thirteen years, Sim did have her last born except that it was not only one last born, but two – a boy and a girl. Said the pastor the day they were dedicated, "And who says that God does not move in a mysterious way His wonders to perform?"

Said Sim's mother, "At last, I can laugh at my enemies. Truly, there is no power on earth that God's power is not greater than."

What more can be added to that?

🎓WAITING

Of course, the production of breast milk has a lot to do with whether a woman has a baby or not. This story shows that it is also not very reliable. At first Sim got pregnant despite the fact that she was breast-feeding "Adequately". Later on, she just could not get pregnant because she was secreting breast milk "Inappropriately"!

This problem is much commoner than people assume. It is due to a hormone called Prolactin. Prolactin levels may be high even in women who are not secreting breast milk at all but then it would prevent the woman from naturally ovulating and having a baby. This might be so even though the woman is menstruating normally and regularly.

Could the family planning injections that she was taking have been responsible for this aberration?

Possibly. The injections were another type of hormone that simulated pregnancy. It deludes the body into thinking it should not possibly get pregnant on top of an ongoing pregnancy. However, the injections were highly unlikely to be causing her the problems two years after discontinuing them. A more likely culprit could have been the Indian and Chinese herbal medications that she was taking, not knowing their exact content nor their exact functions. They might not have started the problem themselves, but could have worsened it, or caused it not to resolve on time. These things have their own potencies. Even Mama's concoctions would have done something but who knows what?

Most likely, Sim had a brain tumor that was also giving her the headaches and visual problems. Fortunately, such tumors are benign (kind) and are amenable to medications.

Sometimes however, they can grow very large, causing other problems especially with movement and vision. When this happens, they would need to be operated. They could also turn cancerous.

It was in treating this tumor that Sim got pregnant. That was why the doctor asked her to continue on the medications for longer.

Another cause of inappropriate secretion of breast milk is the use of some medications, especially some psychiatric medications, and some anti-hypertensive medications.

The problem might not recur in Sim. Sometimes, a permanent cure seems to take place after the pregnancy. If they do recur, Sim would have to go back on the medications, and since these are fertility medications, she had better be warned to be on a reliable form of contraception if she did not wish for more babies.

131

INDEX:

TREATMENT OF INFERTILITY

Infertility (or sub-fertility as it is increasingly being called now) is adequately treated when a woman has become pregnant, carries it to a reasonable length of time, delivers, and takes her baby home! That is success. Below are the general treatment methods in orthodox medicine. They are by no means exhaustive. New treatment methods are also coming up every day.

<u>1. PREVENT IT</u>

Prevention, it is said, is better than cure. Since most of the serious causes of infertility is due to illicit sex, sex should be contained as much as possible within the boundaries of marriages with the partners remaining faithful to each other. It is said in some circles that all girls have sex, and whereas the good girls end up with babies, the bad girls end up with diseases!

This is a lie of the devil. It is certainly not true that all girls have pre-marital sex. Most girls still marry as virgins, having had neither babies nor diseases. Some other hapless girls still end up with both babies and diseases. Some that tried to abort also end up with infertility as well. Some even lose their lives.

The story, *Pre-nuptial Lessons* show that it is not only girls that should remain chaste. Boys too may also catch diseases and not only also end up with blocked tubes but also transmit the disaster to their loved ones. **It is best to abstain**

The World Health Organization tells us that this is prevention only at the primary level. At the secondary level, once any disease is detected, there should be a PROMPT and ADEQUATE treatment.

"Wait and see" wrecks more havoc. Sometimes even when the disease appears cured on the outside, it is really festering on the inside. Syphilis especially does this. There is no room for waiting to see what might happen or foolishly hoping that the problem goes away by itself. The sooner it is treated, the better.

Treatment should also be adequate. The habit of going to the chemist to say "Please mix me some medications" should be totally discouraged. It does not help matters. Equally bad is the habit of discontinuing prescribed medications once symptoms have abated, or due to unpleasant side-effects. What happens in such a case is that the remaining organisms regroup with a vengeance. Having "learnt the ways of the medications", they become more resistant so that subsequent treatments become more difficult and more expensive.

As Ifu was correctly counseled, for treatment to be completely adequate in such cases, the sexual partners have to also be treated whether they have any symptoms or not. This process is called contact-tracing.

2. DO NOTHING AT ALL

A couple is not really said to have fertility problems until they have been trying for a period of twelve months to have a baby. They must be having sexual intercourse at least three to four times a week, without the use of any form of contraception (natural or artificial). The man must also be able to attain ejaculation each time.

Within a full year of trying, many couples tend to achieve conception. A few more will do so in the next twelve months too, without any further intervention. It is not every time that a man has sex with a woman that pregnancy can occur. Pregnancy is only likely to occur around the time that the woman is ovulating. **Most** women ovulate fourteen days **before** their next period begins. The remainder ovulate just before, just after menses, or with no stated pattern at all. Even among those that ovulate fourteen days before their menses begins, sometimes something may happen: pressure at work, change in weather, emotional stress etcetera. With such events, they ovulate when they were not expecting to. Even the stress of speculating on when ovulation might happen might cause it not to happen after all.

A good counsel is for couples to have sex normally and naturally, at least every two days. They are then likely to catch that period of ovulation without even thinking about it. People in ancient times did not have all this knowledge, and yet they had multiples of pregnancies. This was their secret.

3. CHANGE OF LIFESTYLE/ HABITS

There are some conditions that are not conducive to conception at all. Thorough vaginal douching in women especially after sex is very bad. Alcohol consumption in men hinders erection. It also discourages the formation of normal sperms. So does smoking, even when one is just a passive smoker (inhales the smoke produced by another person). There are so many poisonous things in cigarette smoke that affect the major organs of the body, including the reproductive system.

God has so made it that the scrotum, containing the testes, should hang loose from the rest of the body. This is because their function of producing and storing sperms require a lower temperature than the rest of the body. The use of tight clothing, synthetic underpants, sitting down for long, and exposure to direct heat as happens in some occupations like in welding, smelting, smithing and so on, would cause them not to function optimally.

Working with some chemicals like industrial dyes and some petrochemicals also have adverse effects on sperm production and function.

In women, some cosmetics and shampoos penetrate the skin. The ones that have steroids in them tend to interfere with the hormonal environment of the body and could prevent conception.

Recently, cellphones, microwave ovens, laser printers are being implicated but much of these are still speculations, and not really proven.

4. DIET AND RELAXATION

Whereas "Junk food" is not definitely known to affect reproductive functions, the resultant obesity is a cause of many problems. On the other hand, eating healthily with enough fresh fruits and vegetables, as well as adequate proteins is known to encourage the formation of healthy sperms and eggs. Recently, people have touted food products like fish oil, avocado pear, walnuts, some herbs etc. This author has not really had any experience with these but why not, if they are not harmful? One must however be careful about what one takes. It is good to follow only one treatment regime at any given time. A lot of good can also get undone. "Laughter is a good medicine". A healthy lifestyle must include time for relaxation and winding down. Indeed, when sex follows naturally on laughter and relaxation, conception is more likely to occur. People that are very uptight find it more difficult to make babies.

5. MEDICATIONS

There are various medications for the treatment of sub-fertility based on the cause. Some of these medications are hormones that are meant to encourage the reproductive organs to perform as they should. Some medications augment the functions of the organs that are not performing optimally. Some reduce the performance of those that are over-doing it. Some medications "remind" some organs to perform. Others actually supplement for some that are not there at all, or that have forgotten what they are meant to be doing.

Not all medications used for treating sub-fertility are hormones or affect hormonal functions. Some are supplemental vitamins or minerals. Since the cause of sub-fertility differs from person to person, even so the medications used in their treatments differ too.

All medications have their side-effects. Before the patient commences on these medications these side-effects are usually explained. Many women are motivated to continue with the medications no matter how unpleasant the side-effects are. The drop-out or discontinuation rates are mostly among the men. It must however be mentioned that some of these side-effects can be dangerous, and even life-threatening. It is not proper to take these medications without adequate medical supervision. Obviously when side-effects like the development of breasts or shrinking of the testes in the male occurs the doctor must be alerted immediately. Things like deepening of the voice or the development of facial hairs in the female should also be reported immediately.

There is a group of women that get pregnant but lose it quite early anyway. This causes them to become unsure of whether they actually did become pregnant or not. They keep treating for inability to conceive whereas they really should be treating for inability to sustain pregnancy. This is in another group altogether. It has a special treatment of its own. That is why it behooves every woman to keep a chart of when she sees her menses for each month, and how long each period lasted. This is probably the first, and the most significant step in treatment.

<u>6. SURGERIES</u>

Sometimes medications and injections are just not enough for treating the problem. Operations may become necessary especially if there is a blockage somewhere.

IN FEMALES

The operations on the female may be something simple that can be done from the vagina especially if it is related to inadequate menstrual flow. Hydrotubation (The layman's flushing of the tubes) is a form of operation. It has given good results in some women. Sometimes, it may be "breaking down of adhesions", and inserting a loop or a catheter to make sure that they do not recur. Sometimes it could even just be opening up the mouth of the womb to be sure the sperms can get in.

Major operations are called for if there are fibroids (See *The Tales of Ten Women*). The tubes may need to be reconstructed. Accumulated pus or "Bad water" may need to be removed. It must be stated that the fact that one had undergone an operation does not necessarily guarantee success. Many doctors still leave operations as a thing of last resort.

IN MALES

In men, the reconstruction of the tubes can also be attempted. In them though, usually, when the tubes get blocked, there is a tendency for the body to start producing anti-sperm antibodies after some time. This means that the opening of the tubes may not totally resolve the matter.

Men might also be required to undergo testicular biopsy in order to determine the level of the problem. Overgrown veins (varicoceles), hernias, and hydroceles (abnormal bag of water surrounding the testes) are also treated by operation. Afterwards, fertility has been known to improve. The prostate, if enlarged is also removed or rather reduced.

All these are not without their own problems and side-effects.

7. MODERN ASSISTED REPRODUCTIVE TECHNIQUES (ARTS)

With increase in knowledge, the sperm from a man can be extracted, as well as the ova (eggs) from a woman. Both are made to meet in a Petri-dish outside the body. The resultant fertilized egg is then implanted back into the woman's womb to grow and develop. Since the breakthrough that resulted in the birth of Louisa Brown over thirty years ago, this method has been refined and improved on a lot. Newer methods have been introduced. Other methods are still under research. Some centers. claim very high success rates though the methods of grading success vary a lot. Some centers use pregnancy rate. Others use baby-take-home rate. Here are listed some of the more popular and better-known ARTS:

A. ARTIFICIAL INSEMINATION

In artificial insemination, semen from the man is washed and filtered. It is then re-introduced into the woman's vagina and nature allowed to take its course. The semen could be got from the husband or from a donor.

The husband's semen is used in such a way if he is not present, had it preserved before under-going a treatment that would destroy the areas that usually produce the sperms, or is paralyzed and had the semen collected artificially. This method is also used in HIV-discordant couples: that is one partner is positive, and the negative status of the other partner has to be preserved but they still want to have babies.

Donor semen is used when the husband has no viable sperm in his semen. The donor may be someone that is known to both, either, or none of the partners. There is a lot of speculation on whether to call this adultery or not. Some argue that having not had the sexual act, that

adultery is not involved here. *What then would some modes of medical examinations be called?*
Artificial insemination with donor sperms still raises a lot of questions: morally, legally, ethically, and so on. But it is still very widely practiced.

B. INTRA-UTERINE INSEMINATION

This is still a variant of artificial insemination. It could involve the husband's semen or a donor semen still. The difference lies in the fact that instead of just depositing the sperms in the vagina to find their way, the vagina and the cervix are by-passed. The semen is actually deposited into the uterus, as close to the tubes as possible. The essence of this is to by-pass any factors in the passage that might have been dealing adversely with the sperms before. It also shortens the journey of the sperms in getting to the egg. The usual journey made by a single sperm through the female genital tract in order to reach the egg is said to be as much as a man swimming the Atlantic Ocean from the African coast to the South American coast! Intra uterine insemination aims to shorten this journey a lot.

C. IN VITRO FERTILIZATION (IVF)

In In-vitro fertilization, the sperms from the man, and the eggs from the woman are mixed inside a Petri dish. When fertilization has occurred, some of the resultant zygotes (fertilized eggs) are then re-implanted into the woman. Usually, two to four of these are used. The rest are either stored or discarded. This process by-passes many of the natural pathways. It is the best treatment for a woman with blocked tubes, or a man whose sperms are not fast enough.

In most cases, it is the sperms and the ova of married couples that are used. However, in other variation, the sperm, the ova, or both could be from donors. The zygote could even be a donation.

D. INTRA CYTOPLASMIC SPERM INJECTION (ICSI) AND CLONING

ICSI and cloning are the most recent publicized advances so far.

In ICSI, the "Immature" sperms are aspirated into a needle-like apparatus after adequate preparation. This is then injected into the primed egg. The resultant zygote is incubated for some time, and then re-implanted into the womb.

The proponents of this claim that *most* of the babies turn out well. *Some* develop medical problems sooner or later in life. This is not surprising. By-passing the processes of natural selection is apt to have such consequences of passing along some genetic abnormalities.

The theory in Cloning is that every living cell in the body is capable of beginning to grow again, and could eventually become a fully grown human being. What is done is that a living cell from a man or woman (usually a white blood cell) is primed. It is then injected into an egg cell from which the nucleus has been removed. When it begins to show signs of growth and adaptation, it is then re-implanted into a prepared womb and allowed to grow into a full-term baby.
Sheep and some other animals have been cloned. Some scientists claim that they have also been able to clone human beings.

E. SURROGACY

If sperms, eggs or even zygotes can be donated or bought, why not a womb?
Surrogacy is like renting a womb. It really involves the life of the person whose womb is being "rented".
What happens is that a couple that is unable (and sometimes unwilling to) go through the rigors of childbirth, gets someone else to do it for them. Usually, the genetic matter (the sperm and the egg) would belong to the commissioning couple. Sometimes though, the surrogate is expected to also contribute her own egg.

Every pregnancy is a risk to the carrier. That carrier nevertheless, is expected, at the end of all that risk to sweetly relinquish the baby, collect her money, and disappear!

In one celebrated case, the woman refused to relinquish the baby. She claimed that she had become emotionally attached to the baby while carrying it. She chose to rather return the money.

This author also knows of a case in which the woman started bleeding dangerously during the pregnancy. She had to have an emergency Caesarean Section to save her life and that of the baby. After the baby was delivered, she did not stop bleeding until her entire womb was removed. This sterilized her forever!

Recently, in order to eliminate the sense of commercialization of the Surrogate's life, as well as the moral and legal battles, couples are now getting their relatives to be the surrogates. Hence, grandmothers are implanted with the zygotes of their daughters and sons-in-law. Sisters are implanted with the zygotes of their brothers and sisters-in-law and so on.

Recent advances are researching the use of artificial wombs, and animals as surrogates!

F. ADOPTION AND FOSTERING

What many people really want is someone to love, that would love them back. They long for someone that

would make them feel responsible and dependable. Out
in the world are also many children looking for a parent-
figure that would love, nurture, and protect them. Could
these two groups not connect?

Fostering is like temporary parenting. There are many
children whose parents are not fully there, maybe due to
pressure of work, schooling, sickness, one thing or
another. People also take in other people's children to
help with housework, baby-sitting, or such. They are
actually fostering such children at this period.

In fostering, the real parents still have a stake in the
child. Some foster groups form very strong attachments
to one another so that the periods of separation to return
to the real parents become quite agonizing on all sides.
This could be quite frustrating, but wise parents do not
give up. They give it all that they have, no matter how
short the liaison might be. The ties so formed could last
for life. After all, even with one's own biological
children, there also comes a time when the nest empties.
Adoption on the other hand is a more permanent
arrangement. The child is taken in and legally made a
member of the family "Till death do us part" even
though there **might** be no biological relationship.
Surprisingly, a lot of people do not believe in adoption.
They feel that they cannot really relate to someone who
is not carrying their own genetic matter. Some others
say that there would be no filial loyalties and they are
not sure of what problems might arise in the future, and
whether they would be able to bear it for one who is not
their own biological child. Said one woman, "If he

should go through those difficult times that adolescents usually have, I don't know if I will not chase him away from the house. I might take it from my own son but from another person…"

Such arguments do not really hold water. One's biological children are also liable to misbehave. There are increasing cases of Patricide and Matricide in the world today, especially in the so-called developed countries of the world.

Of those who have no objections to adoption, they would rather adopt very young babies. In fact, the younger the better, "So they would feel that we are really their parents…"

This author once heard of an orphanage where the older children pray for God to send them parents that would come to adopt them. People that get parents this way are less likely to abuse the privilege or to take their parents for granted. This is unlike those who did not pray to get the parents that they have.

Increasingly however, there is a global reduction in the number of babies that are up for adoption. In developed countries, abortions are encouraged instead. It is made very cheap, even government-sponsored, or subsidized. That means there are hardly needy babies up for adoption.

As criminal as it is, people pay school girls to get pregnant and have babies for them – another form of surrogacy perhaps!

Someone once said that nobody needs to be infertile these days. A lot can be done but as a Yoruba adage puts it: The secret of a delicious pot of soup is in how much money went into it!

Those who have the money and are persistent enough can always make a baby when the going is tough. Is it not best, however, to strive to preserve one's fertility and to take what God gives free of charge?

BOOKS IN THIS SERIES

THE TALES OF TEN WOMEN (*Fibroids)*
THE BATTLES OF TEN WOMEN (*Cancer*)
THE BURDENS OF TEN WOMEN *(Infertility*)
THE SORROWS OF TEN WOMEN (*Losing Unborn Babies*)
TEN WOMEN IN TROUBLE (*Dying in Childbirth*)
TEN WOMEN IN JOYOUS PAIN (*Operative Deliveries*)

www.ingramcontent.com/pod-product-compliance
Lightning Source LLC
Chambersburg PA
CBHW071438130726
47997CB00006B/2135